Eggs for Young America

The Katharine Bakeless Nason Literary Publication Prizes

The Bakeless Literary Publication Prizes are sponsored by the Bread Loaf
Writer's Conference of Middlebury College to support the publication of first
books. The manuscripts are selected through an open competition and are
published by the University Press of New England/Middlebury College Press.

1996 Competition Winners

POETRY
Mary Jo Bang, *Apology for Want*
judge: Edward Hirsch

FICTION
Katherine L. Hester, *Eggs for Young America*
judge: Francine Prose

Eggs for Young America

KATHERINE L. HESTER

A Middlebury/Bread Loaf Book

Published by the University Press of New England

Hanover and London

MIDDLEBURY COLLEGE PRESS

Published by the University Press of New England, Hanover, NH 03755

Printed in the United States of America

5 4 3 2 1

CIP data appear at the end of the book

For Mark

Contents

Acknowledgments

Grateful acknowledgment is made to the following publications, in which some of these stories were first published in slightly different form: *The Indiana Review*, "Labor"; *Prize Stories: The O. Henry Awards 1994*, "Labor"; *Cimarron Review*, "Alarm" (as "The Sky Over Austin"); *American Short Fiction*, "Grand Portage."

The author wishes to thank the Texas Center for Writers for its support.

Eggs for Young America

Alarm

The American Alarm Associates emblem—an eye—is everywhere. It stares up from the garish advertisements printed on the back pages of the paper. It peers from the corners of the windows in the residential neighborhoods, affixed to tiny metallic stickers that explain: BEWARE. It's emblazoned on each panel of Tyler's work van: a slightly squinting eye, the words PEACE OF MIND arched above the eyebrow in navy blue, AMERICAN ALARM ASSOCIATES stenciled underneath. The eye is much bigger than life-size, it's bigger than Tyler's head, and sometimes, in the mornings when he walks out into the driveway, it gazes toward him in a manner he finds sinister. It seems to him the eye is always watching, like the video cameras he puts up in houses out by the lake, in people's boat garages. At night, it's blank and vacant like a turned-off television screen.

Tyler is dreaming that both his hands are wrapped in tangled coils of copper wire. The house is still, and Holly, beside him on the bed, completely quiet. Branches stroke the rusted window screen; something—possums, he's told Holly when she asks him—scratches in the chalky dirt below the pier-and-beams.

But tonight, he isn't sure just what it is that wakes him up. The possums, or the wind. It has to be one or the other, but suddenly it seems to him that it's the staring, painted eye instead. As if it's gazing through their flimsy bedroom walls. As if it sees him on the bed, his face turned toward the darkened window. The eye's aware he lies awake and hates his job; it knows how, during the month he worked on the system at the First Hibernia Bank, he thought of stealing. It knows he dreams of wires, long and thin and merciless. Behind his closed eyes they turn into something else. Thin strands of something, shining. Barbed wire, or something that gleams, dangerous, like needles.

"I'll kick your motherfucking ass," someone cries abruptly out on the street. The sound of a dropped bottle slides faintly through the crack where the window and the sill don't meet.

Tyler turns over heavily on the bed, and further down Siesta Street, whatever's under Mary Anne's house is keeping *her* awake. It spits and snarls and bumps its body against the asbestos-covered pipes beneath the floorboards. Its claws chatter against the boarded-over hole in the bathroom. It scrabbles at the closet floor.

"What is it?" Opal cries drowsily from her bedroom. "What's that noise?"

Mary Anne would like to think the house is settling.

"It's nothing, honey," she calls through the doorway. "Go on back to sleep."

Close to dawn, the vagrants crunch cans efficiently in the parking lot behind Tyler and Holly's house. Sometimes they build a fire. One of them has wild, goatish eyes. He used to stop Holly when she went into the laundromat, looking straight at her and cursing when she wouldn't give him money. There was another one she got so she could recognize, he always fished for quarters in the empty washers. "I got a hot line to the CIA," he'd tell her, every time, if she made the mistake of raising her eyes to meet his.

"He just *might*," Tyler said thoughtfully, the night he and Holly met, the night they left their laundry in the dryers and went off to eat dinner. "You never know."

This morning, the crackle of a radio blends with the angry crunch of cans.

"What's that?" Holly whispers, rolling over on the bed to touch Tyler's arm. He jerks awake and reaches on the floor for his pants, his head tilted to one side.

"The bums?" she asks.

"Ssshhh," he tells her. "The police. A megaphone." He holds up his hand, his body tense.

STOP RIGHT NOW, the voice out on the street demands. *TURN A-ROUND SLOW-LY*.

Tyler starts toward the front of the house. "Stay here," he snaps at Holly. "Stay back." She drags the sheet off the bed and wraps it around her. It trails along the floor as she walks toward the living room.

"Stay back," Tyler says again, over his shoulder. He's at the window, peering through the blinds. "It doesn't matter now," he tells her, after a minute. "They've got him pinned up against your car. But what if they started shooting at him? Bullets go through walls, you know."

"Oh," she says. How can they prepare for bullets that slide through walls, planes that might fall out of the sky and through the roof? It suddenly strikes her as funny—that Tyler would worry about her but go striding into the living room himself, as if he were protected, as if something about being male made him bullet-proof.

"They couldn't *really* go through walls," she says.

Tyler's work van must be immaculate.

His uniforms are supposed to be immaculate as well.

Such details, the upper management of American Alarm

Associates has decided, make their clients feel much more secure about the amounts of money they are spending. Management has passed this philosophy down to their employees, who receive docks in pay if they cannot keep up appearances. When Tyler gets home from work in the afternoons, his ugly polyester work shirts are smeared with dirt and sweat and greasy-feeling spiderwebs. He only has three uniforms, which means he has to wash clothes at least twice a week. He used to be better about this than he is now. He thinks it might have been because he lived alone. It might have been because sitting in the laundromat watching the vagrants with their ratty bedrolls and their dogs, their quarts of beer and cigarettes, was better than being by himself.

It might have been because when he went to do his laundry he almost always saw the same woman, a woman who folded her clothes carefully and slowly, her profile intent: a woman who turned out to be Holly.

"I never thought," she says now, thoughtfully. The shirt Tyler is pulling out of the closet as he gets dressed seems slightly grayish, grubby. "I never thought there'd be a time when ring-around-the-collar would be something *I* would think about."

"These shirts are impossible to clean," he tells her. He sticks his arms into the sleeves. "Other places do your laundry for you, but not AAA."

Holly watches him. "You're not going to wear that, are you?"

"Yeah," he says. He shrugs.

She turns toward the dresser. "They fired Jeb for not having a professional appearance," she mutters.

"They fired Jeb for something else," he reminds her. "For parking a work van outside The Good Times Lounge after he got off work." For drinking beer in an ugly concrete building underneath the highway on the bad side of the interstate. "There were customer complaints."

"They could fire you for something else and blame it on your clothes."

"If they decide to fire me," he tells her, "the state of my uniforms won't help me."

Holly frowns off into the distance at the bottom of their bed. "If you get fired," she says slowly, "what will we do then?" Her eyes are worried. Tyler is familiar with this look. It means she's adding up the money they spend in her head—in a minute, she'll decide they don't have enough for him to buy a second cup of coffee on his way to work, or that they will have to become vegetarian because they really can't afford to pay for meat.

"Do you get paid today?" she asks abruptly.

"Yeah," he tells her. "I was thinking maybe we'd go out to eat or something. Do something nice."

"We can't really afford it."

"It's my paycheck," he tells her curtly. "Why don't you let me decide?"

He asked her out the fifth time he saw her at the laundromat. It was a Saturday night and her face looked tired under the buzzing fluorescent lights. She was wearing a green-checkered flannel shirt with missing buttons and a pair of worn-out Levis. They were the only people there.

"You must live in the neighborhood," he said. It was right after he had quit everything, drinking, drugs—he never had smoked cigarettes—which was one reason he was doing laundry on a Saturday night. "I see you around a lot," he told her. He wasn't sure how to talk to someone without suggesting going to a bar.

"I've seen you around some, too," she said. "You've always got a lot of laundry." Her smile was shy.

Asking her out to eat seemed to be the best solution. "Have you had dinner?" he asked her awkwardly. "Want to go around the corner to that Chinese place while our laundry dries?"

Holly looked him up and down. Her eyes studied his face. He could tell she was thinking maybe it wasn't really safe to talk to someone she'd met in a laundromat. But maybe it was less safe to stand there in the laundromat with him, alone. In the restaurant there'd be other people.

"Okay," she said, finally. "I guess."

In the end, most of their courtship took place where they went first: the Happy Eggroll. It was the only restaurant Tyler could afford with any regularity. And he wanted to take her out, to be romantic, wanted things with *this* girl to be different from the way they'd been before, back when he was drinking, when anything that happened between him and someone else slid from the beginning to an ending with amazing rapidity.

After work, when he got dressed before he picked her up, he carefully put on a tie. He figured she might laugh but he wanted to be formal. *This is not something to fall into,* he wanted to tell her. *This is something to take seriously.*

When they went to the Happy Eggroll, he and Holly leaned across the sticky table. They stared into each other's eyes. It didn't matter that the eggdrop soup included with their meals was a frightening, bile-tinted yellow. Tyler's hair was always plastered back against his scalp, still wet from the shower. Holly wore bright printed dresses with skirts that swirled around her chair legs. One night, Tyler looked carefully across the table at her. She was saying something, moving her bony hands above her menu. He was amazed that she seemed to want to be with him. He realized she was the only woman he had been with when he was absolutely, completely sober since he was probably seventeen. The thought unnerved him so much that when the tiny, smiling waitress stood in front of the table with their plates of garlic beef, he lunged toward her awkwardly and knocked the plates onto the floor.

The houses on Siesta Street cant to one side, as if all they want to do is slide down the hill into the dirty creek. Mary Anne looks at the bushes in front of her windows carefully when she locks her front door. To see if there are large-sized footprints scuffed into the hard-packed dirt beneath them.

"What are you looking at, Mama?" Opal asks.

"Nothing," Mary Anne says. "A cat." She hustles Opal toward the car.

The sun is barely up above the trees, and Opal is sullen because she has to carry her lunch to school in a plastic grocery bag. She yawns and turns her face toward the car window. She would have rather had, she told her mother airily when she was fixing her lunch, a Catwoman lunch box.

"I hate you," she says to her mother now. Her mother doesn't look like other mothers; she doesn't wear a bra. Her hair is wild and red around her face.

"You'd better not," her mother says. "We're in this thing together, kid." She yanks open the car's hood and prods the solenoid with a screwdriver until the engine roars to life. When she gets back in, Opal will not turn around and look at her.

"Meow," Opal says. She's Catwoman now. She's wearing something long and black and shiny. She's climbing up the walls and leaping from roof to roof. The car swoops down the road leading toward the elementary school. Opal makes her eyes all narrow. She can see what hides behind the bushes. She can scratch their eyes out with her hands. Her mother honks the horn when they pass Tyler and Holly's house. Opal stops being Catwoman for just a minute.

"I'm going to live with Tyler and Holly," she announces to her mother.

"Sure, honey," her mother says.

"They're happy all the time." Her mother turns and looks at her. "Except when they're fighting," she amends.

Tyler's van is lived-in: the front filled with coffee cups and maps, the waxed paper that comes wrapped around honey-dipped donuts, the books he tries to read during his lunch hour. When

he drives up the hills that slope toward the lake, the mess goes
sliding back. When he drives down, it all slides forward.

The house he's working on emerges from between the stunted
trees. Its windows sparkle in the sun. It's designed to be a castle on
the Rhine. The house next door to it looks vaguely like a French
chateau. Both of them back into the chalky limestone cliffs. They
overlook the wide, flat, blue-green lake. Tyler taps his horn three
times before the gate that rears across the lovely, curving driveway
swings back smoothly.

The couple who own the castle on the Rhine are concerned about
their things. When Tyler knocks at their kitchen door, they look
at him warily, concerned he might take them. They only let him
into the house after he's proved he is an American Alarm Associate by showing his ID.

"This system cannot show," the woman says immediately.
"And remember that we have a dog." A gnarled Hispanic man is
running back and forth, dragging a bright green hose across a
wide expanse of lawn Tyler can see through the leaded, medieval-
copy windows. When he walks into the house, the barrel-shaped
dog tries to dodge his legs and disappear across the brilliant lawn.
The husband sits at the kitchen table, frowning slightly, sipping at
a cup of spicy-smelling coffee.

Tyler realizes that these people do not like him in their house.
The salesperson from American Alarm Associates who comes out
first always explains that he is bonded. It doesn't matter, they
don't *want* to trust him. They would not dream of offering him a
cup of coffee. He goes back down the steps and starts pulling
spools of wire from the truck. They hover in the doorway, watching. Suddenly the husband beckons him back inside.

"We've had many workmen out here lately," he says. He clears
his throat. His eyes dart around the bright, high-ceilinged kitchen.
"And we would prefer . . ." He looks toward his wife. "We would

prefer it if you went down to the 7-Eleven at the entrance to the subdivision, should you need to use the bathroom."

Tyler stares at him.

"It's very clean," the woman tells him. "And air-conditioned," she adds. She and her husband look at one another. They both begin to speak at once.

They have to leave for work but their dog is just an *inside* dog. He must not be let out. And the parquet floor in the living room is very old. It is very valuable. It was removed from a house in England and imported. Work boots scratch it up. Could Tyler take his off? The woman's voice is soft and almost diffident.

"You know how it is," she says and then she shrugs her shoulders, her palms turned up and empty, pointed toward the ceiling.

Mary Anne is a Merry Maid. Except that isn't what she tells people if they ask her what she does. She just tells them she cleans houses. It would sound so stupid to say *I am a Merry Maid*. Like something out of one of Opal's fairy tales.

As a Merry Maid, she cleans houses for women who have careers. The women's high-heeled shoes snap efficiently across their houses' wooden floors. When they walk around giving her instructions, they tilt their heads to one side to fasten earrings to their ears. They gaze around their houses, but their voices are abstracted. They clutch polished leather briefcases to their chests. "Your money's on the kitchen table," they tell Mary Anne, and then they leave for work.

Mary Anne likes the first part of the mornings best, when there's still expensive coffee left in the gleaming coffee makers. She likes the smell of furniture polish and the way the sun slants through the kitchen windows. She turns the radio up loud, tuned to the campus station. She sits behind the desks in the women's office rooms and surveys their papers. She sits down on their floors and reads their books.

Mary Anne writes poetry in her head. She sings along with the radio. She makes up songs that she can play softly, barely strumming, on her guitar after she gets home, after Opal goes to bed, after everything is quiet. Most of the songs she makes up are blues.

Woke up in the morning, and the blues hung down in tatters round my bed . . .

There is a stocky muscular man whose band sometimes plays at the nightclub around the corner, down on Travis Street. Sometimes he gets down off the stage and saunters through the audience. He sings without a mike. One night, he stopped in front of the table Mary Anne was sitting at. This was back just after Luther left her. She was trying to get back into circulation.

I'll take you out driving honey, he promised, *out where the road house'll never close.*

He stayed with her a couple of times, nights when Opal stayed at Luther's. Then he just quit calling.

I heard the trains down on the trestles, Mary Anne makes up, *and oh lord I just hung down my head.*

The only rooms she really hates to clean are the master bedrooms. The two hollows pressed into the matching feather pillows. The views of the sunny, landscaped gardens.

The customer, American Alarm Associate training sessions explained to Tyler when he first started working for the company, is always right. Which is the reason why he's working in his stocking feet. There's a hole in the toe of one of his white athletic socks. His feet slide across the polished parquet floor. The house is completely quiet. The matching discreet-blue Mercedes have careened up the curving driveway. The dog is asleep somewhere in one of the rooms Tyler was instructed not to let him into. Tyler lugs his tools from room to room, installing motion detectors in the corners and pressing glass-break sensors onto the windows, hidden behind the drapes, where nobody can see them.

His beeper buzzes against his waist. He sits down on the bed in the master bedroom and reaches for the telephone. When he gets through to Holly, her voice is smooth and syrupy, the receptionist voice he hates because it isn't her at all.

"Did you beep me a minute ago?" he asks her.

"Yeah." Her voice sounds preoccupied. He can hear her fingers strike her computer keyboard.

"Don't type when I'm talking to you," he instructs. He knows she's sitting, slouched down in her posture-perfect office chair, her eyes glued to her terminal.

"Sorry," she says. The typing stops. "It was slow around here earlier. I called to see if you could get away for lunch."

"No way," he says. "I'm way out here at the lake." He lies back on the bed.

"Nice house?" she asks.

"Oh, yeah. They've got this dog. I bet it cost a mint. It looks like a little hippopotamus." He pauses. "They told me not to use their bathroom."

"Why?"

"I guess they think I'll mess it up," he says. He shrugs, although he knows Holly can't see him. He picks his feet off of the floor deliberately and puts them on the creamy-colored satin comforter.

"Fuck them," Holly whispers to him.

"They've got a bunch of porno movies," he tells her. "I found them stashed up in the closet in the bedroom when I was running wire." He stops. "But this house is really beautiful," he says. "You should see the view. Everything's so clean. I saw a deer on the way out."

"Is it sunny out?" she asks him. He squints out the window at the scalloped lake.

"Yeah. It's nice."

"Oh, well," she sighs. "I guess I'd better go."

He can see one of the Mercedes coming up the driveway.

"Yeah," he tells her. "See you." He puts the phone down and stands up. He walks down the stairs. The woman is standing in the middle of the kitchen.

"I always come home for lunch," she tells him brightly. He knows it isn't true.

"Well," he says. "I'm going to go eat mine."

Usually his appearance soothes them. He looks so all-American. He has such blue eyes. Gilt-white blonde hair. He speaks English fairly well—for a laborer—for someone who wears a tool belt slung down low over his hips. For someone who sits inside a van at lunchtime, eating soggy peanut butter sandwiches out of an Igloo cooler.

Holly stares at her computer screen.

"Did you see *Star Trek* last night?" David, the office manager, asks her, standing in the doorway. She raises her eyes. David clears his throat. David often tells her about whatever *Star Trek* episode was on the night before.

"The episode where they're all caught in a loop in the space-time continuum?" Holly shakes her head. David looks at her disappointedly. "What we have here," he tells her. He pauses dramatically. He purses his lips. "What we have here is an identical situation . . ."

It seems that the new receptionist in the outer office has had to schedule a doctor's appointment during lunch. "Would you eat lunch in," David asks Holly, "and answer the phones?"

She's not quite sure how the receptionist being gone relates to *Star Trek*, but David's voice is calm and measured. His demeanor resembles Captain Picard's. Holly realizes he sees their office as the *Enterprise*. Day to day, he guides it through a galaxy of difficulties. Since turnover in the office has been high, Holly is now his right-hand man. *His Mister Spock*, Tyler has suggested to her, laughing. Holly knows she won't get overtime if she works during lunch.

David looks at her sharply. He reminds her, gesturing with his arm in a way that includes each of the fourteen stories of the building they are sitting in, that they are all in the service of mankind. Although they might not realize it. When he says this, Holly understands that he is giving her some kind of warning. What he means is that the ponderously turning wheels of the state government will cease to turn—will seize up completely like the transmission on her car—if she does not give up her lunch hour.

"Just for today," she says, "okay?" She's afraid to ask for compensation time. David nods.

"We have to pull together," he tells her expansively, and when the phone starts ringing, he slips out of her office.

Mary Anne has gotten into the habit of coming home for lunch. She peers back at the alley behind the house when she parks her car. She stands out in the middle of the street and looks down at Tyler and Holly's house to see if anything looks like it's been disturbed, if any of the windows look like they've been broken. When she walks up the sidewalk to her front door she can hear the radio. She keeps the dial turned to a talk-show station. Sometimes it even fools *her*. It sounds like a man is standing in her kitchen. She finds it hard to press her hand against the door and step into the house.

At 2:45, about the time of day he usually started drinking, when he was a drinking man, Tyler takes a break to go to Builder's Square for a box of wire staples. The checkout line he's in moves slowly. He tries to position himself under one of Builder's Square's giant ceiling fans. He could build him and Holly a house just with materials from here, he thinks; it's full of everything they'd need, from boards and shingles to hot water faucets. He'd build it high up on a hill, with cottonwoods around it, where it could catch the breeze. Somewhere where the climate is a little more hospitable. If they just had some land, he thinks. But then he remembers the house one of the guys he works with bought for $90,000. It isn't even very nice. Certainly not worth all that money. The trees around it are spindly twigs, and by the time they're grown, everyone—Tyler, the guy, an entire generation—will be dead. When the guy had Tyler over for a beer, to show off his new house, he flung open the front door proudly and knocked a hole into the inside wall. If Tyler was going to build a house, he'd want to build it out of things that wouldn't break.

Holly's been back at her desk for half an hour when David returns from lunch. David is often absent from the office, although somehow he's there just enough to know everything that happens. Holly suspects he has a spy. He claims that he leaves early, or arrives late, or doesn't come in at all, because he is attending special workshops organized by the state, workshops where he learns exactly how to manage his employees. He nods benignly when he says this and it's true—he's learned how to give pep talks at eight in the morning, before the phones start ringing wildly. Holly swears his speeches are patterned on the ones Captain Picard gives the *Enterprise* crew. The pauses come in the same places.

The few times she's had to call in sick, David's listened to her reasons with a sullen silence. She's certain it's a technique he learned from his workshops. *Last night someone broke into our house. They smashed our bedroom window. I have to stay until the landlord gets back with a pane of glass,* she had to say a month ago. He didn't say, *Oh my I'm sorry to hear* that or *You'll be a little late? We'll do just fine.* When the receptionist, the one who finally quit, called and said, *I'm sorry, one of my kids is awful sick,* David just pursed up his mouth—Holly could see it from the outer office—and replied, *Why don't you get a baby-sitter?*

Because nobody is overseeing him, it's quite possible for David to leave the office for the day at three forty-five. Quite possible for him to practice golf swings behind the closed door of his office and have the undersecretaries hold all of his calls. He spends a good part of the day staring out the window of his office at the dome of the state capitol, the bluish, hazy sky.

When Tyler walks out into the blinding parking lot in front of Builder's Square, his tool belt drags against his thigh. Everything is neatly arranged—electrical tape, screwdrivers, various sizes of wire cutters. The tool belt is a nice one, of pretty decent leather. Holly gave it to him for Christmas.

Once—it seems like a long time ago but it really wasn't—back before he even knew her, before he got cleaned up and got the job at American Alarm Associates, Tyler pawned his tools and belt and Skil saw for ten crinkled five-dollar bills. Fifty dollars. The pawnshops always knew just what amount to offer. The amount you needed to be able to buy whatever it was you had to take. That saw should have gone for more than twenty bucks.

But there were lots of tools in pawn shops. Lots of belts stained dark with sweat. Replacing them was not a problem. Tyler had figured he'd just go back for another belt, when he got the money.

Pawnshops were one of the things he'd learned about only when he had to. He wonders if other people—the people who are whipping their shiny cars around his work van on the highway—even know these things exist.

There are places that serve free meals without asking questions. There are furnished rooms you rent by the week. You can turn an iron into a hot plate. There are things that you discover you can sell when you don't have much of value. The tools you use to make a living. The blood inside your body.

Tyler himself has never had to take a handout. Never slept outside at night. That's what happens when you slide past the edges into something else. Then, he supposes, there are things you sell beside your plasma.

He always recognizes the places where people live when they're busy sliding downward. He sees them on his way out to the lake, when he is high above them on the upper level of the highway. These people never call American Alarm Associates for burglar alarms. The cars in front of their houses are always junked. There are discarded needles in the parking lots and someone always dealing in an apartment around the corner. These are the kinds of places where Tyler used to live.

It comes down to this: you either get clean or you don't.

Tyler severed all his old connections.

You pull yourself up by your bootstraps, and then you get rewarded.

When the guys Tyler worked with stopped by to tell him somebody had something and they'd be glad to get him some, he had to learn to just say no.

He lay on the floor in a furnished room for two days, his face mashed up against the gritty, worn-out carpet.

Now, he can't even be around someone who has the marks running along the inside of their arms. He closes his eyes if there's a needle in a movie.

"What is it?" Holly will ask, looking over at his face, her hand inside a box of stale popcorn when they're at the Dollar Movie. "What is it you're thinking?" That's when he only shrugs. There's no way to explain it to her. It is a precipice she doesn't want to be reminded of. A gap between them they pretend is never there.

When they first moved to Siesta Street, one of the neighbors showed up at their front door, sort of like a Welcome Wagon. He told them they should just call him the Cosmic Cowboy and explained that no one bothered the guy who was living in the storage shed across the street, although it was best to keep their windows locked. There had just been six burglaries, a rape, a peeping tom.

"Just thought you should know," he told them helpfully. They had hardly unpacked their boxes. He leaned his head conspiratorially toward them and stared at their empty living room. "Be careful with your stash," he warned.

"Our stash?" Tyler repeated. "We don't have one," he said flatly.

The Cosmic Cowboy winked at Holly. "Yeah, okay," he said. "So you don't have one. But every break-in there's been, they've found their stash. It's weird," he said. He lowered his voice and looked around. "It's almost like they're watching. In one place they ate a pie. In another, they sat down with a six-pack and watched the TV before they stole it." He looked at Tyler and Holly. "Could you shoot someone like that? If you walked in and found them?"

Tyler shrugged. His hand was on the doorknob. "Thanks for letting us know," he said politely. He started pushing shut the door.

"Hey," the Cosmic Cowboy said, "no problem. Want to come over to my place for dinner next Saturday? A sort of welcome to the neighborhood? Y'all seem all right."

There was a pause.

"Okay," Tyler said finally. "I guess." He looked at Holly.

"Sure," she said and shrugged.

They shut their door as the Cosmic Cowboy walked down the driveway, craning his neck back to look at them.

"He seems lonely," Holly said.

"He seems like a freak," Tyler answered.

"Harmless."

"Harmless," he agreed. He sounded skeptical.

It wasn't until that first weekend that they discovered just exactly how the Cosmic Cowboy was employed. During the week things stayed fairly quiet. But throughout the weekend, cars pulled up to the curb, one after another. The drivers left the engines running. Bikers congregated next to the swaying fence between the two houses, flipping cigarette butts out toward the curb.

Holly peered through their curtains at the steady stream of customers. She looked at Tyler anxiously. Her eyes dropped to his arms before she caught herself and suddenly she wished they were living somewhere else, one of those neighborhoods they could not afford, where the lawns rolled out to the street like carpets and even in the middle of the summer they stayed green.

When Mary Anne was seventeen she had just gotten stoned during a pep rally at her high school in Dallas and walked away from everything. She clambered up the on-ramp of the interstate. When the cars pulled over she told them her destination. It slid across her lips like chocolate, hash, the smoothest brandy: *Austin*.

After that, a very complicated part of her life had started. That was when she had lived in many different places. For a while she had lived with someone inside a VW van. That was when she had met Luther. Now, she's not sure whether to look at those days with embarrassment or some kind of weird nostalgia.

The women she works for don't know any of this, but they look at her critically when she comes in to work for them in her ragged Oat Willie's T-shirt. Sometimes when they come home from their jobs, she's sitting on their front steps taking a break. Smoking a cigarette. She can tell by the way they sidle past that they're embarrassed. They can't believe she doesn't wish she was like them. They suggest things to her. They give advice. Their husbands will help her when she needs to fix her plumbing. Right now, Mary Anne's landlord is threatening to evict her. One of the women she works for is a lawyer.

"You have your rights," she says to Mary Anne. She leans toward her seriously. "I'll help you out." The lawyer wants to pay

Mary Anne back for cleaning up her house, for picking her husband's underwear up off the floor, but after awhile her guilt will probably get lost underneath all of the other things she has to do. This is fine with Mary Anne.

She knew she was going to rent the house she found on Siesta Street as soon as she saw it. She ignored the lime-green paint, the sagging ceiling in the hall. She and Opal wouldn't have to share a room. She stood in the middle of the street and surveyed the dusty yard. The figure of a man traveled slowly down the street toward her. The sun was right behind him and he looked like a scarecrow.

"Hey," he said when he got up to her. "What's up?"

He stood beside her and looked at the house.

"You gonna rent it?"

Mary Anne didn't answer.

"I guess you know," he told her, "it has bad vibes."

"I'll fill it up with love," she countered. She'd smoked half a joint in the car and she felt optimistic. "I'll erase any bad karma. It's so cheap. Two-fifty for a whole house. It's the only thing I've seen I can afford."

The man shook his head. His long, stringy hair was tied back with the twist-tie from a loaf of bread. His eyes were bleary.

"The lady who used to live there, she was bat-shit crazy," he said. Mary Anne raised her eyebrows. "Into bad shit." He looked at her.

"I wouldn't try to raise a little kid here," he said suddenly and clearly. "Who knows what's buried in the yard? She cast spells, you know? Animal sacrifices? The house always smelled funny."

"I don't think that's true," Mary Anne said. She looked down the street, hoping he would go away. The sky was sullen and stirred up and brassy. The other houses on the street were locked up tight. No cars passed them.

"Thank you for the information, though," she told the man. She focused her eyes on his Hawaiian shirt.

"No problem," he whispered. "Just want you to know where things are at." He squinted at her. "But I guess you're going to take it, huh?"

Even though she didn't believe a word the Cosmic Cowboy said, she had plans to buy blue paint, to paint the eaves and shutters and the door frame blue. To ward off any evil spirits. She was going to go down south to the herbaría to get some Home/Health/Happiness cleaner to pour into her mop bucket when she cleaned the house completely. That would negate any of the house's former influences. These were things that she was going to do, but something always happened. The car kept breaking down, and all those things cost money. She tried to nail the windows closed. She wanted a porch light that worked. She talked to the landlord.

"I might have to raise the rent," he warned. He was the shortest man Mary Anne had ever seen; almost doll-like, no bigger than a jockey. His brown face was etched with heavy lines, his hands were gnarled.

"Most of my tenants understand they can't have everything for the prices they're paying." he explained.

"It's not like I don't know that," she said sharply. "I just want a porch light." She looked at him.

"We'll see what we can do," he said. She knew he didn't mean a word of it.

Tyler turns into the parking lot between the square brick building on the corner and the Happy Eggroll next door. The wide eye on the panel of his truck is mirrored in the greasy plate-glass window.

"Hey," he says when he walks in.

"The regular?" Mr. Pan inquires. "One Tiger-and-Dragon Fight, one Orange-flavored Beef?"

Tyler nods. " And four eggrolls," he says magnanimously. "Fortune cookies, too."

"Ahh," says Mr. Pan. "It must be payday. Where is the lady?"

"Not home from work yet. I'm going to take it with me." Tyler reaches in his back pocket. "Umm," he says. "Hold on for just a minute." He leaves the front door swinging. He rummages through the dirty papers on the floorboards of the van. He slides his hands underneath the seats. He pats his pockets down. He turns them inside out. He walks back in the restaurant slowly.

"I'm sorry," he tells Mr. Pan. "I can't find my wallet."

"Ahh?" says Mr. Pan. He raises his eyebrows. He scoops up the plastic Styrofoam containers and stalks toward the kitchen. He doesn't turn his head around to look at Tyler, who is already back out the door and on his hands and knees in the oily parking lot, peering underneath the van.

Holly can remember when the bus was free—but then the city discovered it was the transients who enjoyed it most. The free ride. They idled in the back and soaked up all the air conditioning. Free fares, the city suddenly announced, encouraged delinquency and tempted teenagers into skipping school.

So now the bus costs fifty cents. When Holly climbs on it after work, the passengers that face the front stare at her stonily. A surly man with a faded tattoo spreading across his forearm is sprawled out across the only empty seat. Holly wraps her arms around a pole. The bus jolts forward.

It lets her off in front of a squat, square-shaped building. The neon sign in front explains: THE SHANGRI-LA. This building has no windows, but the front door is always propped an inch or two ajar. The edges of it seem to shimmer in the heat. Holly shifts her purse from one shoulder to the other. Her feet are loud on the dirty pavement. A ragged scrap of notebook paper is taped to the front door. It flutters gently when she walks by. She cuts her eyes toward it.

Come on in, the note exhorts in scratchy ball-point pen, *Our air-conditioning is working. It's cool inside.*

Other days when she's walked past, the note has simply been a terse one: *All ladies busy. Come back later.*

She walks slowly past the barely open door. The stale air swirls around her legs. It smells sort of like popcorn and sort of like an attic. A red, sun-faded velour curtain covers up the barred window set into the door.

The Shangri-La is always running classifieds for new ladies in the Sunday paper.

"What exactly is it they *do* in places like that?" she's asked Tyler. He swears he doesn't know. She imagines that the women walk into little rooms, rolling up their sleeves. Their faces are as blank and removed as if they were kneading bread dough in the back room of a bakery.

Occasionally, one of the magazines left in the break room at Holly's office contains an article which investigates this kind of employment. Call girls are in it for the money, these articles explain. The same goes for topless dancers. They vacation in Tahiti. They wear designer clothes. It's a secret thing they do. Their lawyer boyfriends are unaware of their professions. Walking past the Shangri-La, Holly notices that the parking lot beside it is filled up with cars with dirty windshields and missing hubcaps.

Tyler tries to retrace his steps. The van stalls at a stop light.

"Shit," he says wildly. "Goddamn." He guns the engine. He taps his fingers on the steering wheel.

He pulls into a parking lot and leaps out of the van. WE CASH ALL GOVERNMENT CHECKS, promises the banner draped above the door he heads toward.

"Did I leave a wallet here?" he asks. The cashier looks at him disinterestedly.

"No," she tells him. Her face is moon-shaped and her eyes are fixed on a portable television set hidden underneath the counter.

"Are you sure?" he asks her.

"Yeah," she says. "I'm sure." He stirs his hands through the wastebasket beside the counter.

"Nobody turned one in?"

She shrugs. He thinks it's possible she might be lying.

"Jesus," he says loudly. He looks closely at her. Her face is blank and unremorseful.

"Could I leave my phone number in case it shows up?" She starts to write it down.

"Put down," he tells her, "that I'll offer a reward."

"It won't do any good," she says. Her voice seems smug. She pushes the piece of paper to the side of the counter dismissively, as if to say, *You stupid joe, don't you get it? Your money's long gone.*

Siesta Street curves past the billboards with the smiling graduation faces of the girls who disappear. *Have you seen us?* their lips whisper. Their voices seem to slide across the hot roofs of the cars inching along the road that leads up to the interstate. *Do you know who killed us?* Holly hates to look at them. They're always on the evening news. They're on the front page of the paper. She looks beyond the faces, toward the gray horizon, at the cliffs and the radio towers, red fingers pointed at the sky. Strung out along the ridges of the low, humped hills that ring the lake.

Tyler says the air smells sweeter out there. Out there, it's true, the water of the lake belongs to anyone who builds a house in front of it. And standing on the highway, staring down, she and Tyler have heard the humming of the boats and occasionally a laugh that spirals upward, just like smoke.

She walks along the street as it slopes up from the silty creek that rises with each sudden rain and leaches dry right after, leaving boards and tennis shoes caught up in the brush at the highwater line. Past the Cosmic Cowboy's house and the boats on blocks in his front yard that nudge at the grass as if a sudden hurricane had swirled around them while she was at work and dropped them from the sky. He stands in the front yard, a garden hose dangling limply from one hand as he points it at the browning patch of St. Augustine he's nursed carefully through several burning summers.

"Hey, Richard," she says as she walks past. It's hard for her to bring herself to call him the Cosmic Cowboy, although he's told her he prefers it. He turns and looks at her. He blinks his eyes.

"Hey, Holly," he says loudly. "How much of the state's money did you spend today?"

"Maybe twenty, thirty thousand," she jokes. "Cheese balls and rented plants for senators' offices. I wish it was Friday."

"I got something that would pick you up," he says slyly. "If you and Tyler want to come by after supper?"

"I think we've got somewhere we've got to go," she says. He looks down at the stream of water trickling from the hose.

"No problem," he says jovially. "No problem."

The Cosmic Cowboy got all dressed up for what he called his dinner party. It made Holly feel embarrassed for him. Already she'd discovered he made her feel sad. She couldn't tell what Tyler thought. His face was inscrutable as he sat in the chair across from her at the Cosmic Cowboy's rickety card table. The Cosmic Cowboy had on purple cowboy boots. His head was defined by the lines of scraggly, graying sideburns that crawled down his jawline. Halfway through the meal he'd fixed, he stood up abruptly and pulled a water pipe off the top of his refrigerator. His hair was tied back with the twist-tie from a loaf of bread. He was wearing a yin and yang bolo tie.

"Like," he said, "you know? It's great that somebody else cool has moved into the neighborhood."

Tyler made a noncommittal sound.

"I've been here for years," the Cosmic Cowboy said. "Lived in this house forever. Way back in the thirties, they used to call this area Gypsy Grove. Cause, you know, this was where the Gypsies had their camps. Still sort of the same, you know? Sort of like a carnival. Janis Joplin lived around the corner."

He'd moved to Austin after he got out of the navy. It was the most amazing place he'd ever come in contact with. He remembered everything—the Armadillo and Raul's and Club Foot. He remembered when everybody used to skinny-dip at Pale Face Park, that when the sheriff came up in his boat to bust them, he gave them plastic baggies so they could get their tickets back to shore without them getting wet. The Cosmic Cowboy shook his head sadly. It wasn't quite the way it used to be. Things had started changing when they started building shiny, blue-glass high-rises down along the river. When they started paving up the creeks. When downtown turned into some kind of tourist trap. He shrugged and took a toke from his water pipe. He tilted it toward them. Tyler shook his head.

The Cosmic Cowboy leaned toward them. He had had many occupations. His voice droned on. A june bug rammed itself against the back door screen. For a while, he told them confidentially, in the early eighties, he had done something that involved the three motorboats propped up on blocks in the front yard. The moneymaking possibilities inherent in the boats had dried up in '87.

For a while—and here his voice got loud with pride—he had driven his boatlike Cadillac up and down the highway from El Paso to Austin. The slit and sewn-together upholstery bulged with plastic-wrapped bricks of heroin. To prepare for the run, the Cosmic Cowboy stood in dirty alleyways in Boy's Town and let bathtub speed slide into his veins.

This was back when things like that were easier to do. He always made it back to Austin in what seemed like half an hour. He lived with a chick named SueEllen then. Holly thought his voice got wistful. SueEllen had tied the tie around his biceps for him when his hands shook too much. She had had a purple woven Guatemalan hammock.

Holly pushes open the front door. The house smells like dust and cigarettes. The ceiling sags a little in one corner of the living room. "Tyler?" she says. She hears splashing water from the bathroom. "Tyler?" she repeats. He's sitting in the bathtub, staring morosely at the water.

"How was your day?" she asks him brightly. She sits down on the floor beside the bathtub.

"I could just rob a bank, you know, I know how to do it," he tells her belligerently. He scrubs at his face with a washcloth. He avoids her eyes.

"What are you talking about?"

"I could take everything I know and we could embark on a life of crime."

Holly twists around and looks at him. He slides down in the bathtub so his head is underwater. Holly can't see the expression on his face through the grimy, grayish water.

"What's wrong?" she says. His eyes stare at her blankly. "What's wrong?" she says again. *"Can you hear me? Nod yes or no."* He emerges from the water.

"What did you say?" he asks her.

"Never mind," she says. "Are you hungry?"

"Yeah," he says.

"What about dinner?"

"Peanut butter sandwiches?" he suggests listlessly.

"I thought you said we'd go out."

He turns his head away. "My wallet got stolen," he mutters.

"What do you mean?"

"Just what I said."

"You lost your wallet?" She looks at him.

"Stolen," he says sharply. "I didn't lose it, it was stolen."

"From where?" Her voice rises. "How much was in it? Why didn't you say? First off?"

"Five hundred bucks," he says dully. "My paycheck."

"Five hundred bucks," she repeats. "I told you you needed to open a bank account. And now you lose your wallet."

"I told you," he says slowly, "it was stolen."

She looks down at his arms. He catches the flicker of her eyelids.

"How could you be so stupid?" she says. The words hang in the air. "Goddamn it," she says fiercely.

"Fuck you," he says.

"I can't believe you *lost* it," she says again.

"It was stolen," he repeats. "Why don't you just shut up?" He steps out of the bathtub and yanks a towel from the rack.

"I don't think you lost it at all," she says abruptly.

He whirls around and looks at her. "What are you saying? What exactly do you mean by *that*?"

"Nothing," she says slowly.

His face is red. He shoves it up against hers. "Why don't you just say it, what you think happened?"

Mary Anne's peeping tom was before the first break-in. He stood pressed up against her bedroom window, moaning, until he woke her up. Opal was across town, with her father. Mary Anne peered toward the rusty window screen until she could make out the peeper's silhouette. She ran to the phone and crouched behind the desk in the living room. The peeper moved to another window, crashing through the bushes, so he would have a better view.

"He's watching me right now," she told the 911 operator. "He's doing something with his hands."

While she waited for the cops to come, she thought about the candle that sat on her mantel, the one she'd packed and taken with her every time she moved for years. The candle had seemed funny when she and Luther had gone into the tiny curio shop in Matamoros to buy it. That was when they lived down on the south side and Luther grew pot in a greenhouse he had built in their backyard. LAW KEEP AWAY was written on the glass candle holder in big block letters. There was a picture of a policeman, writing out a ticket, unaware of the Grim Reaper, swathed in black and looming up behind him. Mary Anne had had the candle for so long she'd forgotten what was written on it. It sat there on the mantel, and although it wasn't lit, she was suddenly afraid the cops would never come. Or that when they saw the candle they'd just turn around and leave. There was the sound of rustling in the bushes, as if the peeper had settled down to stay.

Tyler stretches out on his stomach on the bed, his head hanging off the edge. He stares at the dusty floor. Holly looks at him from the open doorway. She turns away and stands in front of the kitchen cabinets. She stares at the shelves. *All that money. Gone, like that.* She grabs things off the shelves and sets them on the kitchen counter. She wipes the empty shelves off with a sponge.

"What are you doing?" Tyler says. He stands in the doorway, watching.

She jumps. "Cleaning the cabinets."

"You think we're not going to have enough to eat? You think we're going to *starve?*"

"I just wanted something to do," she says. Tyler looks at her. His mouth twists sharply.

"Why can't you trust anything? Why can't you trust *me?*"

She bends her head and blindly smooths peanut butter on a slice of bread. She hears the clink of his car keys as he pulls them out of his pocket.

"I'm going out," he says to the back of her head.

She doesn't answer. She just stares at the peanut butter sandwich on the counter as if it's something she'd really wanted, something she thought tasted good.

The first time Mary Anne's house got broken into, they took her food stamps. They slashed the bedroom window screen with something that left shiny marks against the rusty metal.

The second time they simply wrenched the screen right off the rotten frame. They ate what was left of Opal's birthday cake.

The third time, she drove up in time to see them leave. They were walking down the street with four black trash bags. She pulled the car up against the curb and saw a small TV set inside one of the plastic bags. She realized it was hers. She yanked on the emergency brake and leapt out of the car.

"What the fuck do you think you're doing?" she screamed. They turned and looked at her. They were just teenagers, and one of them stared at her with a blank look on his face. His mouth was slightly open.

"You goddamn assholes," she shrieked. They started running down the alley and she followed close behind them. She didn't stop to think at all: if she had she would have been afraid they had a gun, a knife. She wished she had a tree limb big enough to smash their heads in with. She thought she was going to catch up with them. She hadn't stopped to think what she'd do then. Opal peered out the car window, struggling with her seatbelt.

"Mama!" she screamed. Mary Anne stopped abruptly and stood, panting, in the alley.

The first time, the time the burglars slashed the screen to get into her house, they used something sharp, a knife. It was something she had realized at the time but didn't want to admit. They came through Opal's bedroom window. The shiny slash curved upward, like a smile.

*

Mary Anne sits up in bed. There are so many windows in her house. Lately, when she walks through certain parts of it, she smells something awful. Something dead somewhere. And there's something that knocks against the walls. It crashes through the brush in the vacant yard behind the house. It scrapes at the windows and runs along the roof. She slides off the bed onto the floor. The wood is gritty underneath her palms and knees. She crawls toward the living room. If she stands up, whatever's outside will see her. If she reaches for the light and turns it on, that'll only make it worse: from inside, the windows seem blank and dark and she can't see anything but her own reflection, but out there in the dark someone could lean against the rotten window sill to watch her, and the light behind her would shine through her nightgown. She wouldn't even know. They'd be watching every move she made.

She sits on the floor and runs her hand along the top of the desk with one hand until she feels the phone. She fumbles it into her lap.

"I'm sorry," she says into the receiver after she dials. "But could you come over? There's something outside my house again. I can hear it in the bushes."

Tyler's hair sticks up in tufts, pushed back from his forehead into a lopsided pompadour. There's the flash of his tattoo as he pulls a twisted T-shirt over his head while he stands at Mary Anne's front door, Holly close behind him, shoes untied, eyes blank with sleep. He plays the flashlight's beam across the front of the house, over the heavy bushes next to the sidewalk.

"It's us," he says. Mary Anne opens the front door a crack.

"It was in back," she whispers apologetically. "I'm sorry."

Tyler waves the flashlight. "It's okay," he says. "I'll check back there." He moves toward the side of the house.

"I'm sorry I woke y'all up," Mary Anne says to Holly.

"It's okay," Holly says awkwardly. Mary Anne's life is always in some kind of crisis. Tyler emerges from the bushes at the side of the house, a spooked expression on his face.

"I didn't really see anything back there," he says. "Although it's awfully dark. Let's check inside."

They walk through all the rooms but Opal's. Tyler opens up the closets. He shines his flashlight underneath the bed.

"Nothing here," he says. "It must just be an animal. But there's something that smells bad." He wrinkles up his nose. "You smell it?"

"It's bigger than an animal," Mary Anne says wildly. "I hear it every night."

"It must be coons," Tyler explains. "Or maybe possums. We've got them down at our house."

Mary Anne turns toward the door. "Maybe," she says, although it's obvious she does not believe him. "But what about the smell?"

"What I think," Tyler tells her firmly, "is that a family of possums has been living underneath your house. And now one of them's died."

"How can I get rid of them?"

"I guess I could come by tomorrow and we could try to find the way they're getting in. Nail a board in front of it."

"I'd try to pay you something," Mary Anne says. Tyler nods his head.

"We'll see," he says.

"What was it?" Holly asks him when they're walking back to their house.

"Nothing," he says stiffly. "That house should be condemned."

"You looked like something scared you."

Tyler turns toward her. She can barely see his face in the light cast from the streetlamp.

"I," he says. He stops and looks at her, moves closer, so their shoulders touch. "The bushes were bent back," he says. "Like something had been in them. And it was fucking *dark* back there. I couldn't see a thing."

"Just hold the flashlight," he tells her curtly. "Once I find out if there's anything in there, we'll board it up." The back of Mary Anne's house smells of wet wood, of dirt and rotten leaves. Tyler crouches and peers into the hole in the foundation.

"I'm going to have to try to get in there," he says after a minute. " I can't see from here. Hand me the flashlight when I tell you." Mary Anne sits in a sagging lawn chair in the back yard, biting her lip nervously. Holly's body is pressed against the side of the house, flattened between it and the tangled bushes. Tyler lowers himself onto his stomach.

"Don't go in there," Mary Anne calls to them, as if she just now thought of it. "What if they have rabies?" The dirt along the house's foundation is covered with junk; a broken china plate, beer cans, a bone. Tyler tosses the bone out into the yard. "A human collar bone," he says and laughs.

"Maybe you *shouldn't* go down in there," Holly says. She's talking to the soles of his shoes. There's a rusty Tonka truck beside his foot.

"Hand me the flashlight," he says. His voice is muffled. Holly crouches down and sticks her arm into the hole.

"You got it?"

"Yeah," he says. "It smells real *bad* . . . It smells real fucking bad down here." His voice breaks off. "God damn," he says. "Shit."

"What is it?" Holly asks him. He backs rapidly out of the hole. His hand is clasped above his eye. Blood seeps through his fingers. His face looks shocked. He lowers his hand and stares at the blood on it. "Oh, shit," he says. "It doesn't really hurt, but what if it's my eye?"

Holly crouches down beside him. "Let me see," she whispers. "Go get a towel," she instructs Mary Anne. "Look up at the sky," she tells him. A tiny flap of skin curves in a half-moon by his eyebrow.

"Can you see?" she asks. "Can you see out of it?" He squints and nods. Blood drips in his eye. He winks it away. She holds his head between her hands. His hair is matted on his forehead.

"What was it? A nail?" she asks. "There's a lot of blood."

"Head wounds," he reminds himself. "They always bleed a lot."

"Should we see if it needs stitches?"

He shakes his head. "Just clean it out real good." His eyes are wide. "Really, as long as it's not my eye . . . It would be awful if I couldn't see."

"It doesn't look deep," she says. Their heads are close together. She presses his hand.

He looks at her and blinks his eyes. "Okay," he says. He sighs and looks over at Mary Anne, walking toward them. He leans closer to Holly. "There's definitely something down in there," he tells her quickly. "Something that smells bad."

"Like what?" she whispers.

"A dead animal? It has to be. But it gave me the creeps. Don't tell her. I don't think there's even any way to get it out. I'm not going to go back down in there for anything."

Gauze and tape bulk above his eyebrow. Holly's sitting on the front steps beside him, Mary Anne looms over them. Her hands are on her hips. She stares off down the street.

"It's going to rain," Holly comments absently, looking upward.

"Rain," Mary Anne repeats. "Yeah." They can see the Cosmic Cowboy down the street, standing in his driveway.

"It's going to get his car," Tyler says. "It always rains the day he washes it."

Mary Anne *knows* there's something underneath her house. She stares at Tyler and Holly, noticing they're holding hands.

Sometimes, they yell at each other so loudly she can hear them from her bedroom. *I'm leaving,* Holly screams. *I'm going somewhere else,* Tyler will vow. The sound of it slides through the walls of Mary Anne's house. It makes Opal cry. It just makes Mary Anne feel tired. She and Luther had been like that. It was so predictable, the way people swung apart, then came back together.

Luther had nailed their windows closed, so they would not get robbed. He brought her slightly wilted daisies he got for half-price at the florist's when they were about to throw them out.

Some nights, in the spring, he'd take the claw end of the hammer and pry the windows open. They would lie there on the bed; the wind pushed back the scarves she used as curtains. It smelled of dirt and leaves and the honeysuckle that swarmed feebly over the drooping fence. It smelled of the rain that held off in the hills that ringed the city and the lightning reaching down toward the radio towers as if they were a prize. The bed was big and sagging, the headboard black behind them. Luther ran his hands over her face. She grasped the coarse dark hair that grew against his neck. They didn't hear the noises that were always on the street.

She looks at Tyler and Holly. "Jesus," she says harshly. "What are you two doing, holding hands? You think this is romantic?" They look up at her quickly, their faces surprised, and Mary Anne turns her head, looks down the street, past the pale pink pickup resting heavily against the curb with one flat tire, past the yellowed newspapers blown flat against the gutters, past Tyler's truck, the painted eye, which stares toward them widely, stupidly, the words printed above it supposed to be a promise—the eye will never blink. Mary Anne squints at it, past it, toward the Cosmic Cowboy. He aims a hose toward his aging Cadillac's curving sides.

Once a month he waxes it in a three-step process that takes him as long as it takes the shadow of the one mimosa tree in the yard to crawl from one end of the driveway to the other. He thinks of it as meditation. He smooths rubbing compound, polisher, two coats of thick, pasty wax across the Caddy's surface. Occasionally he stops, to peer at the sky, to roll a cigarette and place it between his lips. He rubs the Caddy gently with a chamois cloth.

Built of good Detroit steel that bends for nothing. What America was made from. It's what he told Tyler the first time they ever talked about his car. He moves his shoulders, rubbing. He whistles tunelessly. He wipes each drop of water carefully off the gleaming metal. He puts his heart into his rubbing. He leans into his reflection, the fifteen coats of paint he paid for when his finances were better. The Caddy's finish is so pure he can almost reach down into it. He squints into its depths.

He's told Tyler he can remember everything that ever happened to him. He still knows exactly what it sounded like, the noise the tires of the Caddy made against the pavement of all the different roads he's been on. He remembers on the coast of Georgia, he must have been just twenty-two, driving from Virginia Beach to Miami after he was discharged from the navy. There was something in the grooves of the pavement that made the tires sound like singing. The road was dark, a corridor. Somewhere alongside was the ocean, but you couldn't see it.

"Escape," he promises himself. The tree limbs flail against the sky. The wind has started rising, and down the street, Holly, Tyler, Mary Anne—all of them—they tilt their heads, their faces smoothed and pale and waiting, to stare upward at the trees bent back along the roofs, the lowering sky.

Going Down

*D*alton's gun is black and stubby. Dalton's gun is wrapped in a bread sack in the glove compartment. It's what Charlotte sees when she reaches in for the road map, a few miles out of town; she recoils from it as if it were a snake. Dalton barely turns from the wheel to catch her stare.

"Shut that back up, honey," he says. "Go ahead," he tells her gently. "Close that door."

"Why the gun?" she says. "I don't like *that*."

"When Mama died, I got everything. The property in Dothan, the gun she kept for years. The place I'm living now gets broken into all the time. This seemed like the place to keep it."

Charlotte frowns. "You got a permit?"

"Of course I've got a permit." His voice is suddenly crisp and efficient. "You think I'm some kind of fuck-up?"

"Maybe." Charlotte shrugs.

"Yeah," he echoes. "Maybe. Oh ye of little faith. You ever think I might have changed?"

"What are you now, Dalton? Forty-three? Old dogs, new tricks?"

"My age is kind of a sore spot with me," he says.

Charlotte can't figure out if he's joking. She decides to think he is. "And me the one that's in my prime, now," she tells him.

"Yeah," he says. "What happened?" Charlotte doesn't answer.

"Your mother kept a gun?" she asks, instead.

"Oh, yeah," he says. "You *knew* that."

It was something she'd forgotten. "When did she die?"

"Six months ago, the summer." He presses his foot against the accelerator. "Still crazy as a fucking bug, up to the minute when she pulled the trigger."

It all had started with Dalton, who wasn't from Dalton at all but from one of the dogwood-tree-lined suburbs on the outskirts of Atlanta.

"Well, we ran coons down in those woods a lot," he lied, when John Bainbridge said, *Shit, man, I always thought you were from Dalton.* That was on the wide front porch of the house Dalton was renting when Charlotte first met him, the three of them sitting screened in by the bushes, a plastic trash can filled with melting ice and Shaefer beer beside them, one night in the middle of the summer that started out so heavy, over-warm, a *courtship*, Dalton and Charlotte sprawled out on the worn wood boards, his hand almost hiking her dress up around her hips. Dalton stood up, drawled, *Hand me over a beer now won't you honey*, and John Bainbridge looked down at her, over at him, and quirked one eyebrow, mouthing his pronouncement: *jailbait.*

"I'm passing through" was what Dalton told Charlotte when she answered the phone to hear his voice for the first time in six years. His voice was breezy and there was a tick, a roar, through the receiver.

Charlotte was silent.

"Actually," he said. He drew the word out. "I've inherited some property down by Dothan."

"I don't know where Dothan is," Charlotte said finally.

"Shit, Charlotte," he said. "Across the border, west of Blakely? My mom's property?"

"What border?" Charlotte said. She meant, *Why now? After I just about forgot you?*

"Alabama," he said firmly. "We went down there together once."

"Not me," she told him. "That must have been some other girl. We never went down through South Georgia."

Dalton's voice was stilted. "I wanted you to go with me," he said. Charlotte twined the cord from the phone around her hand and took it through the screen door to the porch. The air outside was heavy, and the porches of the houses that traveled down the street symmetrically seemed to be a tunnel, held up by white square-cornered columns and divided by the beat-up cars that rested in the driveways. She turned around and the phone cord wrapped around her. There was a brown and yellow FOR SALE sign in the yard next door, and she could hear someone calling a dog. The tick at Dalton's end of the line got louder. An overheated engine cooling? Someone's pulse?

"If it's on the weekend," she said finally. "I have a *job*. I don't want to miss work for this."

What started with Dalton? He woke her up? He pulled her down? Was it even fair to say she had been untouched before him? *You looked like such an ice-queen,* he had explained after the first time they slept together, *I knew I had to have you.*

She'd worked at the public library, where everything was far too quiet. Her first job. Dalton came in in the afternoons and sat at a table in the corner, reading *Rolling Stone* and Chilton's manuals, books of poetry. She knew because she had to shelve them later. It was the books of poetry that made her sit behind the front desk and watch him. He was handsome and whole, and when he caught her watching him, he grinned. He was reading Byron. The other patrons of the library in the early afternoons were vagrants. They kept their bedrolls on the floor between their feet. They slept with their heads down on the tables. They tied their dogs to the railing out of sight of the library's front door, and one afternoon Charlotte had walked around the desk toward Dalton.

"Could you please put the books you don't plan to check out on a cart before you leave?" she asked him. Her hands were on her hips. She worked at the public library, she was seventeen. That summer she was always hungry. She spent her lunch hours in the break room with the other librarians, who all were *old*, who wore bifocals strung around their necks, hanging from chains. They ate Lean Cuisines for lunch.

What made her think, well maybe *this* will end it, when he finally called her after all that time? It wasn't like she was dying. It wasn't like he was some form of cancer. *I've been in love with other people since you*, she'd always planned the speech she'd tell him if she ever saw him again. *They don't even look like you.* But the people she loved after Dalton—sometimes they moved in with her and then moved out, or sometimes she was the one who just moved on. When she thought back, they all seemed *flat*, transparent layers, and Dalton was the thing that lay there, underneath them all.

She sat on the sofa and waited for him to pull into the driveway, thinking of the things she should have told him when he called her. *I'm old and fat and tired now,* she should have said. *Maybe it's best just to leave it.* But did she really want to leave it? Part of her wanted him to stand at her front door and look at her—both of them would recognize then that, finally, he meant nothing. But then, there was another part of her that wanted to find out he still meant everything. "Shut up," she said out loud. Things were not the way they were in movies. People didn't just come back and pick right up where they'd left off. There were no ties that couldn't just be broken. Charlotte suddenly wanted to walk into the bathroom to study the mirror, to see what Dalton would find out when he first looked at her. But she wouldn't do it. She'd go on this trip with him, but she wouldn't even take a tube of lipstick with her or a change of clothes.

When Charlotte was right out of high school, when she first met Dalton, he had a mirror hanging on the ceiling above his bed. Charlotte kept her eyes closed tight but sometimes she forgot and opened them, and then all she saw was his broad back. She knew the mirror was revolting. *Take it down,* she said. But then when she was at work, she stamped out Stephen King books stolidly and the other librarians talked to her of overdue notices and torn book jackets and the sultry weather. They held books cradled in their arms and shook their heads over them as if they were dirty children. *When I leave here I go sleep in a room where there's a mirror on the ceiling.* She slapped books down on the counter heavily. At noon, Dalton stood outside the shiny plate glass window and mouthed words at her through the glass. His pants were smeared with clay, and it looked like he was telling her he loved her madly. At the library, only two exciting things had happened over that summer. The air conditioning was out for four days. One of the vagrants pushed up the tile in the men's room ceiling so he could clamber up and over to the ceiling above the women's room, where he bored a tiny hole.

After Dalton picks her up, the radio station that's playing in his car, a dirt-brown Cutlass with seats so bucketed that when she first climbed in she felt like she was sitting on the ground, is playing the exact same songs that had always been on the radio, from the time she was in high school and even before.

"Oh, jeez," she groans, when he reaches out a hand to change the station. "It's like a time warp." The radio plays Lynyrd Skynyrd and Steve Miller, Aerosmith, the Stones.

"It's classic rock," he says amiably. When she had answered the door after he knocked, they'd stood there and looked at each other, without a kiss, a gesture, without even a handshake.

"It's not," she argues. "It's just the shit from when I was back in high school. Since when did that get classic?"

"Since eleven years," Dalton says and gives her a slightly dreamy smile that makes her edgy. He looks the same. "No gray hairs yet," he tells her. He drives casually, one hand draped over the steering wheel, and Sweet Emotion is playing on the radio. Charlotte stares out the window; the highway is empty, and she and Dalton might as well be back eleven years, although then he had his truck, the space behind the seat always filled up with his dirty laundry—she still remembers one night, the truck parked at the damp edge of some dirt road, when she'd started crying, and Dalton, after staring stonily out the window, had relented and reached into the back to hand her a T-shirt to blow her nose on.

"Why did you call me?" she asks flatly, but she doesn't look at him, just keeps her eyes firmly on the Pizza Hut, the Golden Pantry, the New Maranantha Chapel sliding past.

"Why did you come?" he counters.

"Unfair," she says. "I asked you first."

"Because I wondered what had happened to you," he says slowly. "I don't know. Because I looked in the phone book and saw you still lived in Harriston, and Harriston's on the way to Dothan."

"On the way from *where*? Where is it you live now?"

"New York City," he says proudly.

"Harriston isn't anywhere between New York City and Dothan, Alabama."

"It is, sort of," he tells her. "You can check a map."

Dalton had been an artist. A guitar leaned up against the wall beside the bed under the mirror. Sometimes he wrote plays. But mostly he was a sculptor. He had watched Charlotte at the library for a few days after she spoke, and then he'd asked her out. "You know," he said thoughtfully on their first date, while she sipped at a margarita. "Sometime, I'd really like to sculpt you." The next week he led her back to the shed behind his house. The shed—*the studio*, he corrected as he unlocked the padlock on the door—was damp and cold although outside it was high summer. The shed was filled with chunks of clay, smeared across the floor like blood, and the smoke from the cigarette Charlotte lit lay like a screen between them.

Two days after that, he took her to the country to seduce her. A picnic lunch he had packed carefully, and wine. They walked on the gleaming black slabs of rock that lined the edges of the river and that was where he kissed her. It started raining. *Struck by lightning*, he said, and Charlotte was only seventeen, she didn't realize what he said was stupid. *Charlotte*, he whispered her name. *Another southern city.* They ate their picnic in the truck and after the second bottle of wine ran around to the back and climbed up into the bed, to lie under the camper cover. That was when she found out he was thirty-two. *I could teach you everything*, he told her.

You have to love it, he'd explain to her later that same summer, every time he took her driving, his hand stretching across the seat to touch her thigh. *You don't even have a choice.* He was talking about the countryside. He kept a ragged blanket in the truck so they could stop and lie down on it, could catch a glimpse of sky. Hemmed in by pines.

Why, yes, Charlotte finally agreed. You did. Because the air was rich, like bourbon. Because the clouds were wheeling by. It never occurred to her that the pickup truck, the farm-boy squint he directed through its windshield at the plowed cotton fields, might just be an affectation. In the mornings, after they drove away from town, he'd stop the truck beside the ditches that ran along the road, and they'd stumble through the looping brambles, stripping the bushes of blackberries. Or on their way home they'd stop beside the orchards and he'd hold the barbed wire up while she scrambled under the fence. Back in the truck, they'd each eat a peach and throw the others out the window. Charlotte didn't even like peaches much; the feel of that fur against her tongue.

Columbus is an army town—the streets underneath the dirty-colored sky are lined with pawnshops and massage parlors and hopeless boarded windows, criss-crossed by the railroad tracks. "We could make it all the way tonight," Charlotte tells Dalton when he turns off the highway to stop at a motel.

"Too dark," he reminds her. "There won't be any power out there," and once they're in the cinder-block motel room, he stands in front of the mirror and studies his reflection: the roses wrapped in barbed wire on one biceps, the bluebird of happiness that perches on the other. LIVE FREE OR DIE, a banner swirls beneath the roses.

Charlotte still remembers when he got the roses—during the second of their five summers. She had stopped working at the library because its hours no longer fit into her lifestyle. By then, she worked across the street from Dalton's house at Cafe Okay, and he worked a few shifts, downtown at Dupree's. When he first got the tattoo of the roses with the phrase unfurled beneath them, the letters had been slickly black. For almost a week the excess ink had seeped into the sheets while they slept: one morning she looked at him before he was awake and the smudged black letters EVIL stared up from the flowered rosebud sprigs that were the pillowcase.

"What jackass said 'Live free or die?'" she asked him, nudging him awake. The barbed wire wrapped around the roses didn't look like anything, you'd never know what it was supposed to be unless you asked him. Dalton yawned and looked up at his reflection on the ceiling.

"I'll make you get one, too," he said, inspecting his tattoo. "I'll brand you with my name."

*

"No new tattoos?" Charlotte says, now, sitting on the lumpy single bed and watching. "No hearts with someone's name?"

"Nope," he says. "Completely single." He leans over the basin toward his reflection in the mirror, and the muscles in his arms are still hard and solid, the same as they were when she was seventeen, nights when he kissed her, placing his palms against the wall, and she, her head upturned, was in between them. She looks away, but before she does, she notices that his stomach hangs over his belt, a little.

"You tired?" he asks her.

"Yeah," she says, looking at the fingerprinted door and dingy curtains.

"Me, too," he says and sighs. "Shit. Exhausted," and there is something so heavy in his voice that she turns back around to look at him. He's slouched in the ugly chair beside the bedside table, the phone book open across his legs.

"What're you looking up?"

He raises his head. "It's just something I do, on trips. Look up people I used to know, to see if I can find them. I mean, there's nothing else to do, no television."

Now, Charlotte thinks, *is when I should say: which one of us should take the floor?* But she doesn't even bring it up, just takes off her shoes and slides under the blanket. She's still awake when he turns off the lamp, lets the phone book thud onto the floor. He gets into the bed beside her; his hand clasps hers, tightly, and then his grip relaxes. He is sound asleep.

The cinder-block motel room is dark and fairly quiet. She's turned facing one side of the bed, he's turned facing the other. Both of them have always had the habit of talking, of moving, in their sleep.

*

So here they are, Charlotte and Dalton, and in her sleep Charlotte is—what?—maybe twenty, maybe nineteen. Dalton's days are full of women who loan him things, bodies and cars.

It's Charlotte's beat-up bike he's chaining to a lamppost in front of the newsstand on the corner, and when she sees him pause and stroke his hair back after a quick look at his reflection in the plate glass window, she knows she wants it back.

"Hey," he says, when he sees her and Jonelle sitting on the curb, sharing a cigarette. He walks toward them. You'd never know he just turned thirty-five, with his high top tennis shoes and Salvation Army polyester pants. Jonelle watches Charlotte, and Charlotte watches Dalton. They're on the curb across from the university campus, and Jonelle has on a beaded ankle bracelet and a toe-ring. She is always barefoot. Dalton has little nerdy spectacles and if it was a different time of day, if it was ten o'clock at night, the frat boys who drive past on their way to the beer-bar might be shouting something at them, *you fucking freaks, you get a job*. Although all of them wait tables in restaurants where the frat boys choose to congregate, although Dalton is a sculptor and the shed behind the house he rents is filled with red-clay sculptures of naked women Charlotte looks at carefully to see if she can recognize the faces, to see if any of them look like one of the other women she sees Dalton talking to.

"Hey," he says again. He never touches Charlotte when he runs into her on the street, just stands back, his hands shoved into his pockets. But still, it seems like he's glad to see her. Although with him it's hard to tell. Jonelle leans closer to Charlotte. She nudges her with her bony elbow.

"Don't hog that cigarette," she says. Charlotte looks up at Dalton.

"Hey," she says.

"Where you been?" he asks her. "I tried to call."

It's what he always says, and Charlotte can't tell if it's true or not.

"I've been around," she tells him casually. "You could have found me if you wanted." Jonelle stands up. The bells on her ankle bracelet jingle.

"I'm going across the street," she says. "I think I see Tom in front of the record store. Is that Tom, do you think?" She squints and neither of them say anything, neither of them turn their heads to watch her go.

"I thought we weren't going to hang out anymore," Charlotte says.

"When did we decide *that*?" he asks her.

"Night before yesterday," she says, "at your house." His face is blank. She's thinking of how he had called her at Cafe Okay toward the end of her shift and said, *Why don't you come on over, after you get done there? I've got a twelve-pack.* How she had found a pair of bright-green lozenge-shaped earrings that wasn't hers on the table by his bed.

"Oh, well," he says. He smiles. His teeth are white and even. He lowers his head and whispers in her ear. "Missed you," he mutters, and then lightly, barely, as he looks off into the distance, his hand brushes her hand.

Dalton had always been an actor. *A liar,* Charlotte accused him sometime after that first summer. *Naw,* he answered back. He talked hunting and the woods as if he were an expert with John Bainbridge, who lived up in a trailer close to Rayle. When he waited tables at Dupree's, he wore a knitted tie. When he drove down to Atlanta, the truck loaded with sculptures he was taking to some gallery, he kept his diamond earring in and put his Converse hi-tops on. When he applied for grants, he looked alert and collegiate. *The secret of the world,* he explained to Charlotte, *is always self-promotion.* And when he talked to women, he always took his wire-rimmed glasses off and looked at them intently. As if their words were valuable. As if he were mining gold.

In the morning, after they leave Columbus behind, the tin roofs of the shacks on either side of the highway sag toward the pastures, rusted the same bald color as the dirt, an ugly orangey-red, and Dalton leans back against the passenger-side door, twisting and untwisting the piece of paper that has the directions written on it, flattening it against his knee.

"You're going to tear it," Charlotte wants to say but doesn't, just asks him, "Does any of this look familiar? Don't you remember coming here before?"

Dalton looks at her blankly. "Sort of," he says slowly, "I mean, a little, maybe." He stares out the window as if hoping for a landmark. "I remember someplace, but I don't think it was this." He'd been leaning forward tensely, but now, all at once, he subsides, sitting back against the seat. What was it he'd said when he called her? *My mother finally died.*

They both are quiet, and Charlotte hunches forward, her fingers wrapped around the steering wheel, staring through the windshield.

Or maybe *this* is Charlotte.

She's twenty-one. Veronica shares the Saturday day shift with her at Cafe Okay. Saturdays are always slow and it is just the two of them, and most of the time they stand out by the kitchen smoking cigarettes. They have a perfect view of Dalton's house. The blinds are all shut; he's still asleep. Veronica thinks Dalton is a romantic. Veronica is older than Charlotte, and she had been one of Dalton's roommates once, when he still rented a room in an old house on Station Street. Charlotte hates Veronica with all her heart.

"Bullshit," she says.

"He is," Veronica insists. "He's sweet. I really think he just wants to get married."

Veronica irritates Charlotte because she somehow seems dumber than she should be, seeing that she's twenty-six. She realizes Dalton has at some time told Veronica his marriage speech.

"If he wanted to be married, he'd be married," she says loudly. She doesn't tell Veronica that she has also heard the marriage speech. That Dalton has sat across from her in a booth at Dupree's, a pitcher of beer on the table in front of them, and said, *I really want to get married. I want to settle down.*

But I can't get too committed to you, he'd explained after a pause. *Because you're so much younger. One day two or three years from now you'd just pick up and leave me.* Standing behind Cafe Okay, Charlotte looks at Veronica and knows she should do something so she will avoid Dalton. Move? Die? She can't think how else to be quit of him. Because there's something about being with him she can't explain. It overreaches everything. When he comes over to her rented room and then they sleep until four, there's something about the crack of brilliant sunlight that edges the heavy blanket nailed up against the double windows. Something about the thick hum of the fan in the corner of her room and the quiet empty hallway outside her door. Everyone else is at work. Tires turn on the street behind the house, chewing at the gravel. A man is standing in his front yard, watering a flower box. Charlotte sees him when she pulls the blanket back from the window. Dalton stands behind her. He presses her up against the wall, the rickety wooden desk. He whispers in her hair, they move toward the bed, and he is walking backward.

It occurs to her that one of Dalton's naked women sculptures looks a great deal like Veronica. She smashes her cigarette out on the asphalt, not caring that the night manager will see it. She can hear the night dishwasher in the kitchen as he clocks in. She walks inside and leaves Veronica standing with her cigarette.

"Goddamn," Malone says to her as he hangs his coat up. "Didn't you girls do a fucking thing today?" Charlotte shrugs and peers through the doorway at the empty restaurant. "How you doing, sweetie-pie?" he tries again. "How's it going?" Charlotte scowls and later, when Malone answers the phone, he doesn't even bother to hold his palm over the receiver. "Charlotte, darling," he yells, "it's lover-boy, all tattooed with the mottos off of license plates." He knows because Dalton has branched out into performance art, down at the club on slow nights. He always takes his shirt off.

This is another thing Charlotte remembers.

One time, Dalton cried, after he came. She hadn't been sure what she should say, so she'd pretended not to notice. Just got up with the sheet wrapped halfway around her and crouched in front of the stack of records beside the record player until she found *Highway 61 Revisited* and slid it out of its sleeve.

The sound of it filled up the room and she got back in the bed beside him.

"What I listened to, the summer I was fifteen," he told her, and she lay back against the mattress trying to calculate what year that had been. 1965. It was the year she'd been born. She couldn't imagine what it must have been like.

"That was the first worst summer," he explained.

It was the summer they sent him to his grandparents in Biloxi. Charlotte's housemate, Davis, was playing Hank Williams in his room. Charlotte's back was propped up against the wall, she could feel the music through it. Dalton reached for the bottle of bourbon he always brought with him.

"You're the only one who knows me, really," he said wildly, later, when the bottle was empty and knocked over on the floor. "I mean, you're *from* here. You know what it's like. And you're so damn smart . . ." But Charlotte knew she didn't know him. His family, his mother, his brother who'd moved to Seattle. She knew that. The asthma that developed the year his parents got divorced and disappeared by the time he was twenty-three. Summers at the beach. His family had migrated down from Tennessee in 1843. All that history. It didn't mean a fucking thing. Although they sat around exchanging it as if it helped explain them. It was barely morning and she nudged him. "I'm not at all like you," she said flatly. "You're crazy." His face was blank and confused.

"What?" he said slowly. "What? What were we talking about? I don't think I remember."

"I don't remember much about when I was little," Dalton says, leaning up against the car door, rain sliding down the window behind his head. "I don't remember hardly anything." Charlotte knows it's not completely true—back when they lay awake all night, reaching for the twelve-pack on the floor, he had told her some things. That he lost his virginity in a suburban living room, and the shag carpet on the floor had left rug burns on his palms and knees. That the summer his mother first tried to kill herself, they'd sent him to his grandparents' in Biloxi, where he played Dylan records over and over. Charlotte couldn't imagine listening to those records when they had just come out and were crawling up the charts, when they were still brand-new.

If Dalton was to tell her about these things *now*, if she hadn't already known them, she would feel compelled to make soothing noises, would think carefully for a response that was correct and understanding. She hadn't had such considerations when she was seventeen. The first time he talked about his mother's suicide attempts, they had been in the car on the way up to the mountains. She'd just stared out the window blankly. When she remembers Dalton talking, she remembers reaching for her cigarettes or for the dial on the radio.

"Do you remember," she says suddenly. *This* is why she's in this car with him. "What happened?" He answers immediately, as if he already knows what she's referring to, as if she doesn't have to say: *why we started to hate each other?*

"I moved," he says flatly. Charlotte realizes that when it ended for Dalton was not exactly when it ended for her. His way may be truer, factually, but she doesn't quite believe it.

"The camping trip," she says, "the one we took right before we broke up, that last summer?" Dalton slouches against the door.

"We went camping?" he asks her.

Or maybe it's that Charlotte is still the Charlotte from that final summer, when she's twenty-two and Dalton is thirty-seven and they are going camping in the mountains, picking a spot below a gravel road Dalton suddenly jerks the truck onto when he spots it from the highway. The road swings in a half-circle before it reemerges between the trees. Below it, a tiny stream slides over chunks of smoothed-off granite, but there's also lots of garbage. Dalton brakes the truck and they get out. He stands in the middle of the road and stares up at the trees. There isn't any noise, and Charlotte notices that a single condom is affixed to a bush that grows out of the ditch beside the road.

"There's no bathroom," she mentions. She's standing next to a metal oil drum that overflows with beer cans. "There's no real shower." Dalton looks at her. He heaves their canvas tent out of the truck.

"Yeah, well," he says. "Didn't you say you wanted to rough it?" He grunts when he bends over to pick up the bundled tent.

"This is better than any state park anyhow," he explains over his shoulder as he walks toward a flat spot down beside the creek. He drops the tent on the ground and stares up the mountain. He puts his hands on his hips. "At a state park you have to pay. And there would be all those RVs," he tells her. "All those old people. And you can't hardly build a fire without somebody telling you where you have to put it. You can't even hunt for firewood."

"This way," he continues, "we've got privacy." He surveys the creek bed. Charlotte scrapes leaves over a chicken bone with the toe of her hiking boot. A logging truck is laboring up the steep grade of the main road; she can hear it through the close-packed trees.

"Okay," she tells him. The creek gurgles cheerfully beside them, and she squats and puts her hands into it. The water is clear and smells of metal. Her hand stirs up the silt against the bottom and for a second the tiny shards of mica look like gold.

While they put up the tent, cars keep turning off the highway and driving slowly down the gravel road toward them. Where they're standing, there's nothing but the rounded rocks in the creek and the sound of trees and Dalton saying hold it like this, but then there's the sound of tires turning onto the gravel road. The aluminum tent poles skid in the spongy dirt and then collapse. The blue and yellow canvas tent settles downward, sending up the smell of mildew. A mud-spattered Buick idles on the gravel road above them. Two blurred faces peer out the windows and down at the creek. Charlotte and Dalton stand and look up at them, and after a while the driver finally puts the car in gear and drives away.

"What are all these people?" Charlotte says. They stand back from the tent and look at it. It droops sadly at one corner.

"Sightseers," Dalton says knowledgeably. "They drive up from Atlanta to look at the changing leaves." Charlotte looks at her watch. It's eleven on a Monday morning, and the people in the car had been watching them. They hadn't been looking at the trees.

The next car that drives up is a nicer one. It pulls up after they get the tent set up, when Dalton has gone off somewhere with his Boy Scout ax.

"Saved all these years," he'd said with satisfaction when he pulled it out of the sagging cardboard box in the bed of the pickup. He ran his finger along the blade and went off through the trees to look for firewood. Charlotte arranges the canned goods they brought on top of the cooler. She lugs some rocks up from the creek to build a fireplace and then sits down on one of them to wait. A car rumbles up the road toward their campsite. It looks like it has just been washed. A man wearing a suit opens the driver's side door. He doesn't notice Charlotte. He walks around to the other door and opens it. The woman gets out and smooths her hair. She wobbles on the gravel in her high-heeled shoes. She looks down at the creek and then says something to the man, who quickly takes his arm from around her waist and shrugs. Charlotte watches them climb back in their car. The windows are rolled up. The engine idles. After a while they drive away.

Dalton walks back into the clearing and drops some branches on the ground. "That's that," he says. "Why don't we go get beer?"

And then their campsite is behind them almost a hundred miles; they've driven through three dry counties. Charlotte looks over at Dalton and his stubborn hair is blown back, the wind from the driver's side window back-combing it so high it almost touches the pickup's ceiling, his fingers almost white around the steering wheel. He's looking at the road in front of them. He won't turn his head. She reaches for the radio.

"I don't think I can stand that shit," he tells her. He draws the words out, snaps them off, one after the other. There are beer cans littering the shoulder of the road, between it and the shiny metal guardrail against the gaping space above the gently folded mountains. Charlotte looks at him and then she lunges forward, sending the last few bars of "The One I Love" sliding off into thick static before she snaps the radio off.

"Why don't we just go back?" she says.

"No." He says it so flatly that there's nothing left for her to do but stare out the dirty windshield at the hairpin-curved road and the truck's humped hood. The highway winds along the ridges, and on the driver's side there's the slippery gleam of shale and underbrush, the mountain rhododendron slanting up the hills no light slopes down. On the other, there's the swift curve of the guardrail. A good view of Slaughter Mountain laid out dark against the light horizon. Blood Mountain is the one they're driving on. The truck points toward the gap between the two, where there's supposed to be a town. The tires slow when the road humps up. They quicken when it pitches down. Dalton's prized hood ornament leans forward, suspended above the grayish highway. The metal hair is frozen, streaming back toward the truck. The cold breasts point toward the white dividing line.

"I never would have thought," Charlotte says, "that it would be so hard to find beer up here."

"How much further is it?" he asks her. His eyes are on the curving road. He won't look toward the view. Charlotte opens up the map.

"I can't tell," she says. "It makes me carsick."

"How far?" he repeats, just like he hasn't heard her. They're down in the valley now, where there isn't a town at all. Charlotte has the window cranked down as far as it will go. The smell of wet wood and dirt and pines slides into the truck. Dalton looks at her.

"How far to the next goddamn podunk little town?" he says. The curly hair lying along his temples is damp with sweat. His fingers drum against the steering wheel.

"Why don't you ask and see?" she tells him, but when he waves down a pickup going in the opposite direction, the old man in it tells him there's nothing before they get over the next mountain.

"Christ," he says. He pulls over at a graveled overlook. A station wagon with backpacks strapped on top whizzes past, the whine of its engine hanging in the air long after it has disappeared from view. Dalton's hands are shaking. "Do you think you could drive?" he asks her finally. He presses the keys into her hand.

"Is it that you're scared of heights?" She backs the truck toward the guardrail. "You should have said before we left." His angular body is curled toward the passenger door panel and his eyes are closed.

"That's not what it is at all," he mutters.

Back then, Dalton said he drank because he was an artist. Faulkner, he reminded her. He said he drank because he was thirsty. "All my family drinks a lot," he told her. "Even if it's just ice tea." These were things he said to Charlotte when they were in town, when there was a liquor store around the corner. "Bourbon's best up in the woods," he said before their camping trip. "A nip beside the fire. Yeah. That's the way you do it." Charlotte didn't respond, just stood at the kitchen counter putting a box of safety matches into a plastic bag so that they wouldn't get damp, up there in the mountains. "But, hey," he said, "we don't really need it. That's just the way it's done, you know?"

"I don't drink anymore," Dalton tells her.

"It doesn't matter to me," Charlotte says. "It's not like we're connected."

"I guess that's why I called you. Because I wanted to say something. That I was sorry. There are a lot of years I can't remember quite."

Charlotte clutches the steering wheel and stares out at the highway. "You said you'd teach me everything. Does this undo all that, the stupid shit you taught me?"

"Christ, Charlotte," he says. "I'm sorry." His tone is petulant and Charlotte knows that he is still an actor, that she is not performing as expected.

"We set up camp down on that turn-around," she says. "And cars pulled up all night, like it was the make-out spot for all of Union County." Camped there in a dirty gouged place in the woods, the ravines filled with beer cans. How can he not remember? It had been afternoon when they got up to Highlands, all the way across the border, and he made her go into the liquor store. *Only get a six pack*, he commanded, and when they finally got back to their campsite it was dark. When he turned the truck so that the headlights would illuminate the tent, they saw it was ripped to shreds. "Shit," he said quietly and sat there with his hands around the steering wheel. Charlotte got out and slammed the door.

Their canned goods had been thrown into the fire. They were swelled and bulged and burned. They had left the embers smoldering, which was stupid, Charlotte realized. They could have burned the mountain down, a shaved bald scalp without its trees, and after that it would have looked the same as all the ugly orange land outside Atlanta. But she was not the one who was a Boy Scout. She was not the one who claimed he had run coons down in the woods. "Well, *fuck*," she said. Dalton was bent down on the seat of the truck, fishing underneath it.

"Do I have any beer left?" he asked her.

"Rednecks?" she asked him, ignoring his question. "It was definitely people who did this."

Dalton threw the truck into gear. "I'm going down the road," he said. She thought he meant, to find a ranger. "The lake we passed? That campground? I bet they have beer."

"Don't you remember?" Charlotte says again, "don't you remember any of it?" But now Dalton is asleep, his head lolling against the window, and it's been hours since they crossed the border into Alabama, since they left behind the bright blue billboard painted with a bulbous peach, the words *The State of Adventure*.

When they pull up to the house Dalton's mother left him, there's a faded NO TRESPASSING sign tacked up over the front door; there isn't any driveway. Dalton's awake now. Charlotte parks the Cutlass in the middle of the street. "It doesn't matter," he says. "There're probably only three people living in this fucking town— I doubt any of them will drive in this direction." The house is across from railroad tracks and faces a sprawling antebellum one. "Renovated," Dalton says, "Probably lawyers from Columbus."

The yard is littered with the pods from two gnarled magnolia trees. The pods look like hand grenades, the waxy scoop-shaped leaves are slick underfoot. The magnolias arch, touching the rusted roof, unkempt, barely letting any light in.

"Jesus, Dalton," Charlotte says. "I had no idea you'd inherited something like this." She steps up on the wrap-around porch, craning her neck back so she can see the turret dripping with wooden gingerbread. Dalton is still sitting in the car.

"This is genuine Victorian," she shouts back to him. "You got the key? Let's go inside."

She's peering through the dirty windows when she hears his step behind her. "Dalton," she says. "This staircase. Maybe mahogany? Or heart-pine? You always hear about that. Absolutely termite-proof." She turns toward him. He's jiggling the key in the lock, hunched over; he clutches his jacket together with both hands.

"I never really knew the grandparents who owned this," he says slowly. "My mother's side. She always said she'd been disinherited. I guess not completely. She ended up with *this*." He looks with distaste at the rotten floor boards of the porch. "Who knows how long it's been empty. I only came here once before, and back then she had tenants." He fumbles with the key. The door is warped and sticks against the jamb. He puts his shoulder to it and pushes.

The front hall is adrift with leaves. It smells of rot, wet earth, something sickly sweet. There's still a carpet on the floor, a large dark stain spreading across it.

"The roof must leak," he comments. He stands there, staring at the ceiling. Charlotte pushes open doors and looks through rooms. They open in on one another. There's a heap of bottles in one corner of the wide, dark-paneled room that looks out on the porch. The dining room? The parlor? The mantelpiece is carved elaborately, held by columns, the woodwork delicate around the mirror set above it. She can see Dalton reflected in it, still staring at the ceiling—the mirror faces toward the door she'd stepped through, the way they always do in older houses left out in the country: positioned toward the open doorways, to reflect out any bad things that attempt to come in.

The fireplace is small, grated for coal, and faced with light-green mottled tiles. The two tiles in the top corners bas-relief, Grecian-looking profiles. The Victorians, Charlotte thinks, oh yeah, they loved those classic cultures and what is this but Georgia, where the columns still rise up like fingers, burned and scarred all the way to Savannah and the sea? Rome, Sparta, Athens. But they aren't in Georgia anymore; they've crossed the border into Alabama. One of the tiled profiles is male, the other female. The hint of her neck is swanlike and her hair is bound up with cords in some kind of Hebe's-knot. She looks toward the man across the grating, and he looks back at her steadily. Their faces are the same, pure, serene, the chins up-tilted slightly, though his is slightly coarser. Charlotte pushes open the far door and steps into the kitchen. The linoleum is coated with leaves and the back door stands ajar, rain has been slanting through. Rust stains the sink where the porcelain has worn away under the faucet. On the farthest wall spray paint scrawls out the sentiment: LYNYRD SKYNYRD WILL NEVER DIE. But they did, Charlotte thinks. A plane crash. Although they have new albums out now. She pushes through a door and ends up back in the hallway. Dalton still stands at the other end, beside the wide front door. She walks toward him. His jacket hangs open and in one hand he holds a fifth of bourbon, his mother's stubby pistol in the other.

"I didn't stop," he says. "Drinking. I guess I lied." He smiles and weighs the pistol in his hand.

*

Dalton always said his mother was crazy. Stuck back somewhere else, he said. She smoked cigarettes for years, but never on the street: a lady never did that. They lived in one of Atlanta's pricey suburbs. His mother was a member of the Junior League. When he was nine, Dalton had gone to dancing school. His cousin had made her debut at the Cotton Ball in 1970. But then, when he was in high school, he worked part-time in a factory where they made rope. He bought his first pickup truck. On the weekends he and the guys he'd grown up with drove out of the suburbs and parked their trucks in cowfields and proceeded to get drunk. And after college he became an artist, and saying you were from the suburbs just was not too cool. All big cities were up, geographically speaking, and therefore better, he explained to Charlotte. Atlanta was just a big dull *town*. All those years, he said that he would leave it.

"Stuck," Dalton says. He flicks the safety catch on the gun. "Unstuck."

"What are you planning on doing with that?" Charlotte asks him. She moves toward him slowly. "Hunt raccoons?"

Dalton looks around the dirty hallway. He stares up the staircase that leads to the second floor. "Shoot out the windows," he says blandly. He takes a swig off his bottle. "Shoot out every single one. And then I got three cans of gasoline out in the car." He draws the word out slowly. Gas-o-line.

"It's a beautiful house," Charlotte says.

Dalton shrugs. "Totally infested."

"With what?"

"With shit," he says and spits onto the floor. "And who the fuck would buy it, down here in this stupid town where three people live? There's not even a grocery store. I'll burn it down and then be free of it."

Live free or die, Charlotte whispers. Dalton is still such an actor. "Why'd you bring me along?"

"Oh, *you,*" Dalton says, as if he had forgotten her. "I thought you would enjoy it."

She should have said: *Even a town of three has a sheriff.* Should have said, *And you do have neighbors, they're gonna hear you shoot that gun.* She should have. Should have talked him down from it, the way you talk them off the ledge outside the burning building. The way she should have talked him out of beer, that summer in the mountains. But there are horses you can put your money on, and those you can't. Dalton has always been a losing proposition. Charlotte sidles toward the door. She takes a breath. There is nothing, she reminds herself, that has to hold her to him.

"I'm leaving now," she tells him. "I don't want any part of this."

"Okay," he says absently. "Just wanted to say 'bye,' you know?"

"Well, okay then," she says. "Good-bye."

"For a while it worked, you know?" he tells her. "Back when we were together. The river, and the highway, and the way we used to stop at flea markets and you would bargain the old ladies out of their old clothes? We had a lot of fun." Charlotte thinks he's going to whirl around and look at her, brandishing his mother's pistol, but he's just staring at the leaves that cover the floor, the piles of bottles in the dining room. "I think I'll do that mirror first," he says thoughtfully, hefting the gun.

Charlotte slides through the door and runs down the walkway to the street. There has to be a sheriff in this stupid little town, some Boss Hogg lookalike, but what is it she's going to tell him? That there's a crazy man who wants to burn up his inheritance? She wonders how far back Dothan is and how long it will take her to hitchhike there—Dothan, home of the Trojan condom factory, where there has to be a bus station.

*

After the bus leaves Dothan, rain slants down toward the asphalt and it seems to Charlotte there is something pressing her into her seat. The hard, awkward weight of Dalton's shoulder against her thigh? She shifts and turns toward the window. The shadow of the bus is thrown against the highway's cement retaining wall, looming large and wavering and always keeping pace. She's in the flat, sleepy edges of Alabama, where towns are called Flor-Ala, swathed in Spanish moss.

Roads appear to angle upward or downward on a map, but once you're really on them, they only take you straight ahead. Georgia presses closely against Alabama's borders. Florida stretches and humps beneath them, its water flat as a mirror, palm trees twisting in the salty breeze.

Dalton stirs in his sleep. "No," he whispers suddenly, and then, "good-bye." Charlotte stares through the window. The space beside her on the seat is empty. Outside the window, fences bind the road on either side. What was it they'd grown up hearing? You loved the land you had inherited simply because you had to. There'd been no one to teach them that they had to understand exactly what had been passed down to them before they could begin, at last, to choose.

Labor

Monroe's Hands

*M*onroe's hands are hard and calloused. There's a jagged crescent of scar gouged into the fleshy part between his thumb and forefinger. Where a chisel slipped, maybe. His right index finger stubby and lopped-off. Some industrial accident, he says. A faint hairline of grease under every fingernail. He keeps a can of Go-Jo in the bathroom by the sink, plunges his hands in it when he gets home from work. Twists them under the running faucet but they don't come clean, completely, ever.

"My hands," he says, surveying them bitterly. Dried blood across his knuckles, where he drags them across something. Insulation, wood, roofing, concrete. "My mother always said I had *artistic* hands." He splays them on his thighs. "Shows how much *she* knew." Jane takes Monroe's hand between hers. Trying to make him think of something else. She presses herself into his hands: a road map of every job he's held, the lifeline of his labor.

Monroe's Eyes

Monroe has faint creases in the corners of his eyes. It was what Jane noticed the first night they were together, when he stopped at the corner of a building and bent his head to the flicker of a lighter, cupped in his hands. Like a young Paul Newman, maybe. Vision's shot, he muttered later, squinting drunkenly at the restaurant menu. That night, they squeezed their bodies into his narrow single bed, and he moved restlessly beside her. That much hasn't changed: at night his hands stir the bedsheets blindly, as if he dreams he's running wire. He twitches like a dog in its sleep. "I don't dream," he says flatly, positively, when she inquires. "Those aren't dreams. They're cramps, that's all."

When Monroe gets home from work he turns his television on, in an apartment complex full of doors, huddling toward each other, with blaring television sets behind them. A good location, out near the industrial parks. A free VCR when you move in. It's moving *up*, that's what it is, and the asphalt lot in front is full of dirty pickup trucks and company vans which must be washed every weekend or risk company demerits. At night, the laundry room is always busy, full of bachelors who could be Monroe's brothers: hair receding slightly, the muscles in their stomachs almost washboard smooth, their biceps hard, but getting softer. Labor is a young profession.

Monroe's neighbor's sister drives over to the apartment complex to do his laundry. *What'll happen when he's not so quick, when his back goes bad?* she asks Jane, folding clothes in the laundry room beside her. The brother that she worries over builds highways, their foundations rooted in the bodies of crane operators, welders, builders. Her brother's eyes dream blankly at the alkaline dirt scraped clean, the dust, the wide, white sky. The jackhammer keeps him awake, the thought of four o'clock's six-pack of beer keeps him going. Monroe's neighbor's sister believes in drug testing, George Bush. Her mother had religion. Her brother will be dragged down soon enough. She wants to save him the worst of it: the plunging, snapping, faulty wire, the clutching fingers of the careless co-worker who falls.

Duane, Monroe's neighbor on the other side, he does his own laundry, bewildered. The brown uniform shirts tumble, boneless, in the dryer. He's outside the door, fumbling for a cigarette. "I need me a good woman," he informs everyone who struggles in the door under the weight of their dirty laundry. "One who'll wash my clothes." He used to have a girlfriend but he doesn't any more. Monroe saw him through *that*, the week he moved in without any furniture; the first night, when he stood at Monroe's door, asking if he could use the phone. Monroe handed him cans of Miller out of his refrigerator. The ashtray in the living room filled with half-smoked butts. Monroe went down to the liquor store for a bottle of cheap bourbon. Duane picked up the telephone. Called the house where he used to live and hung up when his girlfriend answered. He circled the living room edgily, turned the bottle of bourbon up until it pointed at the ceiling. Next door, in his apartment, the smuggled-in rat-terrier bitch yelped and moaned, scraped at the door until her toenails bled. The lights were off but the television set was on. From the screen, Tom Cruise surveyed the wreckage of his living room; the radio turned up too loud, the trash can in the kitchen overflowing, beer cans and McDonald's wrappers, all leached pale under the television's gaze. At Monroe's window, Duane stared down at the parking lot. Maybe his girlfriend would change her mind. He took another swig of bourbon. She'd thrown his work clothes out into the yard, the television set, the box of tools, the half-grown dog. She'd said she'd have the dog put down if he didn't find a place to keep her. He looked out at the parking lot. A girl locked the door of a red pickup and walked across the asphalt. "Hey, honey," he yelled loudly. She turned her face toward the window and held up her hand. She pointed to the ring on her finger. Duane shrugged and leaned further out the window. "Why don't you just come on up here?" he instructed. "All I want's a little of your time."

Behind every door a television set is blaring. Monroe says it's education. He watches CNN, public TV. He watches *Cops, America's*

Most Wanted. He leans forward intently when the policemen shove the lawbreaker face first into the mud, the booted foot square on the writhing back. "That's it," he says triumphantly, "that's how it's done." If Jane isn't in the apartment when he gets home, he checks the closets carefully, to make sure she hasn't been hung up like clothes by a bad man, a man like one on *America's Most Wanted*, one who would break into the apartment and chase her past the breakfast nook with a long knife in his hands. It happens. He's seen it on TV.

Monroe's Legs

"My old man," Monroe says. "My old man, all the hair worn off his legs. I'll quit my job before I let that happen."

All those years of wearing polyester pants. Monroe's old man, run out of Baton Rouge and into Houston when he got the goods on the wrong rural policeman. Everyone knows about Louisiana.

"You're *investigating* the wrong place, boy," the three cops who stopped him on the swampy, dark shoulder of the highway told him while Monroe watched, trying to hide his eyes from the glare of their flashlight, hunched over on the passenger seat, his awkward, fourteen-year-old's knees hitting the dashboard.

"*Boy*," Monroe says now, bitterly. The largest cop flung his father's private investigator's license out into the sucking bayou. There was more to it than that, but that was all Monroe saw, that night. It was enough for him. His old man slid, then on, going out to the store for butter and coming back seven hours later.

Monroe's mother never asked. They lost the house, the brand-new Ford. His father swore that he was on some kind of *list*, by God. Bottles of bourbon hidden in the carport and the trunk of the car, in the wheel wells; his father's voice, raving, trailing off, under the yellow lightbulb on the screened front porch, as constant as the crickets. Monroe's mother twisted her hands, bit her lips until they bled. Monroe hunched his shoulders, his arms and legs too big, hands dangling at his sides. Went down to the rotting dock behind the house with his bamboo pole and flung the carp onto the warped boards just to watch them flop. Bringing his foot down on their dull, fishy bodies. Their cold eyes watching his booted foot descend. Not even any eyelids. He wanted them to blink.

Monroe's old man: now he's old, really *old*, and the master of the scheme, the scam. He sniffs them out like dogs do meat. Monroe's mother takes each new one to heart like religious salvation. For a while it's water purifiers he sells door to door. Free enterprise, he calls it. When a customer says he can't afford one, Monroe's father puts his shoulder to the door and patiently explains it. If you sell four you can have your own, well, not for free, but at half the regular price. It's a *steal*, Monroe's old man insists, but it's just a steal for him: he gets the percentage, each time he hooks some sucker in, convinces him to sell them.

"A pyramid, then," Monroe points out softly, in Houston for Christmas day. It's ninety-two degrees outside his parents' apartment complex. His father is brandishing a check.

"A pyramid's fine if you're the point man," he says heartily. He no longer calls up Monroe to say, *Now, son, I got a job that fits you perfect.* Now he just keeps Monroe informed of his running total, as if that will convince him. "Retirement," he crows. "And I'm just fifty-five."

"I mean, there was that, and there was labor," Monroe tells Jane, when they're driving home. "It'd be different if his schemes worked out." He knows that in a month or so his father will be testifying for something new. The Mr. Auto-Fix-it franchise. His father goes up to Dallas for a seminar, to learn how to charge customers for parts they don't need, learning how to cut the largest corner and come out with a profit. Monroe's mother puts dollar bills in chain letters and watches for the mail. His old man has lost three houses now; "*lost* them," Monroe says to Jane, "like they were his car keys!" When they own a split-level, Monroe's mother can convince herself they're still okay. Two cars totaled, forced around the trunks of trees. One repossessed.

Monroe's Back

There's a picture of Monroe that Jane found in a box shoved under the bed, and he can't be more than twelve. His father must be riding high: there's a boat propped up, slantwise, next to the garage. The person holding the camera must have stood at the farthest edge of the backyard. Monroe's father sits at a metal patio table. Monroe's mother is caught beside him, in the act of pouring something from the top part of a blender into the glass he holds up to her. Her hand is on his shoulder and her face is solicitous, wiped smooth. Her high-heeled sandals sink into the grass. Her hair is swept back from her forehead in a stiff blonde dome. There are gaudy rings on each finger of her hand. The look she gives the camera, unsteady in her high-heels, is resigned. As if she knows the rings, the boat, the brand-new Osterizer blender are all about to disappear.

Monroe is in the farthest left-hand corner of the picture. He's sitting on the ground, his knees drawn up to his chest. His back is to the patio table, his shoulders slumped. He is looking at something beyond the scalloped edge of the photograph, not because it's particularly interesting, but just because it's there.

Monroe's Body

Welts all over his body from sweating outside in the heat. His legs shiny where the hair's worn off. His back is going bad. He worries about hernias and layoffs. In the morning, he drinks burned coffee in the warehouse and eyes the chart taped to the door, the chart designed by upper management to record the rise of the most productive worker, the employee who will be recognized as "Top Gun" for the month and rewarded with a ten-dollar bonus in his paycheck. Monroe hasn't been Top Gun for months. One month he called in sick; another, someone called the number painted on the back panel of his van. TELL US HOW WE DRIVE.

"'Tell us how we drive,'" Monroe says. "I know how I drive. Like anybody who has to drive this fucking interstate all fucking day across this fucking town." At least he hasn't gotten a speeding ticket. Then it's drug tests, reprimands. Each employee of the Company has been issued a slick, official pamphlet reiterating the problem of illegal influences: *Watch the employee who wears sunglasses, who has called in sick, who curses over extra hours, who uses "slang," whose productivity is down. . . .*

Monroe knows it could be worse: he could be filling out forms, standing bleary-eyed in lines that snake around the Employment Commission parking lot at seven-thirty every morning. Could stand exchanging cigarettes and small talk with the rest of them, holding their Styrofoam coffee cups with beat-up hands, shuffling forward and then stopping, patient, in a line that stretches, stops, bunched-up until ten, maybe eleven every morning. There's always that. *Displaced workers.* Like the hand of God has scooped them up, shaken them in a meaty fist, and tossed them out, to bounce like dice along the dirty pavement. Staring snake-eyes in the unemployment line. Shook out and scattered, waiting for the wind to pick them up and blow them someplace better. There's always that. There's a bad disc in his back from lifting, stooping, carrying. But it could be worse, he could just be laid off. He stands in the shower after work, leaving a ring of gray grit around the drain. When the water runs down his face it tastes like salt, like sweat, like metal, like blood.

Monroe's Voice

No matter what, Monroe sings in the shower. His voice, it swoops and stalls like the highway across the border, past the dirty customs station, down into Mexico.

"The Baja? Ruins of Spanish forts up in the mountains? Or concrete huts with banana-leaf roofs down in the jungle on the Yucatan side. Tangerines you pick right off the trees." He's seen it in the *National Geographic.* His eyes gleam, bloodshot, weary. His vision's shot, he says. Jane can't see exactly what it is he pictures.

"We could do it. Really. Just disappear down in there and never come back. No one would ever fuck with us, no one would even know just *where* it was we'd gone. I heard it only takes three hundred bucks to live a year . . ." He lifts his beer can to his lips. Catches Jane's stare. "Down there I wouldn't need to drink, honey."

"In Mexico," he continues, "they give you a metal driver's license. So that if your car goes over the edge of some road, bursts into flames, they'll be able to identify you." He lights a cigarette. "Your *remains,*" he says with satisfaction.

Jane's Heart

Jane met Monroe at a party. "What do you do?" she said politely, slightly bored.

"I'm a *laborer,*" he said, crushing his beer can with his hands.

"Well, *everybody's* a laborer," she said brightly. She didn't know a thing.

"But I can sing like anything," he added. Picturing himself on the cover of *Rolling Stone?* Inside the house, somebody put on Patsy Cline. Monroe danced Jane in a circle in the bare dirt, putting his feet down carefully, as if he was balancing them along the steep ridgepole of some half-constructed house, as if they were on a broad, iron, rusty beam and that was all there was between him and the ground. He laid his hands against her back and they were big and certain, warm. She felt the calluses through her shirt.

"I have a bike," he said shyly. He made it like a question. "If you'd like to take a ride?"

*

No matter what, Monroe sings in the shower when he gets home from work. Towels himself off and scrubs fiercely at his greasy hands. Jane's in the bedroom. Her bags are packed. For leaving him, for Mexico? She doesn't really know. There's the hiss of the pop-top of a beer can in the kitchen, and Monroe holds it tightly, in his hands.

The Hat

*A*nna's hat was a pinwheel of ivory-colored cloth roses and she felt inordinately proud because she had only paid a dollar for it at a secondhand store earlier that morning and because, although she had always heard New Orleans was a dangerous city, she had safely negotiated her way from the airport to the Quarter and from the Quarter to the zoo and back on the street car—now all she had left to do was stride up Magazine Street to meet Michael at the Café du Monde. When she looked toward her reflection in the plate-glass windows she walked past, it seemed to her that if she angled the hat forward on her head, she might look like a Chanel model. She felt happy; she was wearing velvet shoes with Cuban heels; when she had tried on the hat in the secondhand store, peering at herself in the wavery mirror behind the jewelry counter, two transvestites rifling through a pile of silky under-clothes on a table had raised their heads and watched her.

"Stunning!" said one. "Delicious!" commented the other. Anna gave them both a wide smile and paid for the hat immediately. Van always said New Orleans was a dangerous, dirty city; he also would have told her, reprovingly, that she shouldn't wear hats she found at secondhand stores—who knew whose head they might have perched on.

For a minute, as she walked up Magazine, where the doors to

the antique stores were propped wide open and behind each gaping, dim-lit doorway, gilt and tarnished silver glittered as if inside
a cave, Anna remembered the dream she had had the night before, back in Houston, when her oversized purse had lain on the
coffee table next to the front door, already full of what she considered necessities for her trip: a toothbrush, her hairbrush, a tube
of lipstick, a change of underwear tucked down in one corner.
She had told Van she was going to Galveston to visit a woman
she'd gone to high school with, a woman she hadn't seen in quite
some time, a woman who, and here she began making it up, had
recently had a child and even more recently had gotten a divorce.
A weekend full of girl talk, she explained vaguely. She would be
back on Sunday.

Then they had both gone to sleep and Anna dreamed she was
lying next to him and it was early morning. The light coming
through the curtains was faint and barely colored. Her hand was
against his side and she could feel each rib, each intake of breath.
He was as thin and nervous as he had been when they first met,
five years before. The indentations between his ribs seemed
strong, unnatural, and with her fingers splayed between them,
they seemed to Anna like the palings of a fence, or bars. She woke
up suddenly, unsure if she had really pulled her hand back.

"What time are you going?" he asked her.

"Nine," she told him carefully. "Why?"

The blankets twitched, and she knew that underneath them he
had shrugged his shoulders.

At the Café Du Monde she ordered a beignet, and when she
raised it to her mouth, the powdered sugar blew back toward her
face, her black crepe dress, her coarse, dark curly hair. A lean
black man prowled between the tiny tilted round-topped tables.
A spoon protruded from the back pocket of his blue jeans. It was
dank and humid and the sky was black toward the river, but the

man had a long-sleeved shirt on, buttoned severely at the collar and the cuffs. The river smelled fishy and Anna's table was shoved up against a pole with a flapping flyer taped across it. The flyer showed a picture of a college student. Anna squinted at the type beneath the picture. The college student had plunged into the river at exactly 12:07 the past Saturday night. He had swum against the current. He had not been seen since then. Anna raised her eyes and looked out at the jostling tourists. A band further down the street was playing "Summertime."

Suddenly, Michael's figure emerged from behind a tour bus. He walked toward her, a shoulder dragged downward by the suitcase he carried in one hand. The double-breasted suit he had on appeared to be a new one, although the pants hung on his lanky frame. It seemed to Anna that he looked a great deal like an extra from a low-grade gangster movie, someone who would be quick to drop his luggage and set up a scam, a quick shell game. She was almost surprised there was not a plainclothes cop behind him. The ridiculous cheap suit touched her. She stood up, straightening her dress. Michael's face changed when he saw her. It was the same look Van had given her, five years before, when he had seen her for the first time. It was the look that always made Anna feel that she was just about to be in love. She removed her sunglasses and turned toward Michael, giving him a slow, wide, inviting smile.

She had married Van the same way she did anything: an idea got lodged in her head and she ran with it. The things she decided about Van might not have had that much to do with him at all, but afterward it was difficult for her to remember what she had made up about him in the first ten minutes after she met him and what had actually been a part of his personality to begin with.

It hadn't hurt that he looked exactly like Paul Newman, completely different from anyone she'd ever been with, with fine, blonde hair and sea-blue eyes. It was sometime after the wedding that she realized it hadn't really been love at first sight. All it had been was that both of them were *ready*; when their paths crossed, they took ideas they'd carried around for some time and dressed each other in them. It had been as simple as imagining someone in a certain set of clothes you thought would be becoming to them. And the way they had met had been the way one *ought* to meet the person one would marry—the details of it were the sort an old married couple would trot out on their silver wedding anniversary, to prove a point that everybody listening would understand. It was fate, that's what the story was supposed to illustrate, and wasn't that what made people fall in love, after all?

Michael hailed a taxi to take them to their hotel at the other end of the Quarter, saying that his feet hurt. He sat against one door, Anna against the other. Their cabbie stuck out his lip and pushed at the buttons on his radio, switching from one tinny religious station to another.

"Bourbon Street," the cabbie said, shaking his head, when Michael told him their destination. "The seat of sin in this wicked city," he added mournfully. Anna wondered if the New Orleans Chamber of Commerce required that taxi drivers exaggerate the city's decadent image. Michael put his hand heavily on her thigh. She looked at him; the suit, the sunglasses.

"I'm still the same," he said cheerfully, noticing the direction of her gaze. "Even in a suit."

Anna shrugged. "I suppose I'm the same, too," she told him flatly.

Michael leaned back on the seat and put his arms behind his head. "Not this weekend, honey," he drawled. "This weekend you're Jezebel. Cleopatra. What's-her-name from *Dallas*." Anna stared at the back of the cabbie's head. He was still shaking it sadly, as if he knew that everything Michael had ever said had been a lie. He reached for the volume knob on his radio and turned the sermon up too loud for any further conversation.

*

Once the taxi deposited them outside their hotel, they nervously eyed the bellhop who led them into the elevator. Michael fingered the roll of bills in his pants pocket. The elevator doors slid open and the bellhop motioned them through, pressing the door open with an outstretched hand.

"Y'all on your honeymoon?" he asked over one shoulder as he led them down the elegant, hushed hallway and an endless strip of carpeting that stretched like a river past the wall of closed doors.

"No," Anna said quickly just as Michael told him yes. The bellhop shrugged, stopping in front of a door and unlocking it with a flourish. He stood aside as they walked into the room. It was airless and smelled of disinfectant and another woman's heavy perfume. Anna sat down on the bed and watched the bellhop as he busily pulled back the drapes and switched on the television set.

"Well, there you are . . ." he said. He put his hands behind his back and looked at Michael. Michael looked back at him and reached into his pocket. The bellhop counted the money and clapped Michael on the back.

"Y'all have fun now," he instructed. The door slammed shut behind him.

From her position at the end of the bed, Anna noticed that he had switched the television set on to an episode of *The Young and the Restless*. Michael walked over to the window and looked out. Anna stared intently at the square-jawed leading man and the big-haired heroine on the screen.

"We got a great view of the garbage," Michael said, clearing his throat. Anna stood up.

"Well," she said. She reached over and turned off the television set.

"Well," Michael repeated and pulled the drapes closed.

Anna could remember all the different ways it had been *before*, before she had gotten married. How sometimes sex had been a surprise, like unwrapping brightly colored packages; how in the mornings she had eaten leisurely breakfasts with men and afterward was free of them. That had been before AIDS, of course, when it was unnecessary to ask so many questions. But even so, there had always been a moment, before they shed their clothes, when they looked at each other hopefully, with some sort of expectation.

And there had also been a time, more recently, when there was something about the things Michael said to her that she was unable to resist. Those words—they somehow soothed her; Van said so very little—for a while had seemed a justification for what she was doing. In the beginning of the affair, she had been shocked to discover that falling into infidelity wasn't one of the most difficult things she'd ever done. She'd always believed herself a dull, serious person, one who weighed every action heavily before proceeding and then took only the most sensible course. She thought she was not spontaneous, that if a stranger were to come up to her on the street and press the keys to a brand-new Cadillac in her hands, she would return them without a second's hesitation.

She realized she wasn't following the prevailing etiquette for a woman involved with a married man. She read her women's magazines—she knew exactly what she should be thinking. In a proper affair, the other woman focused all her attention on trying to convince her lover to leave his comfortable wife, spent her brief moments with him trying to convince him that what he really wanted was to exchange one sort of domesticity for another and settle down with her instead. Anna knew the moment Michael left his wife, or she left Van, would be the moment their passion for each other died. Michael only wanted part of her, she only wanted part of him. It was not the way she was supposed to be. When a woman got involved with a man, she was supposed to submerge herself in him completely. You spent your life honing everything within you for the moment when you found someone. After, of course, you were happy. Or maybe, Anna thought suddenly, all that really happened was that you were drowning and you didn't know it.

Michael's wedding ring was on his hand. Anna's was nestled in a corner of her purse, wrapped in Kleenex. They were wide awake and dressed for dinner, in the elevator going down. Anna's Chanel No. Five perfumed the air. Michael's hair, still damp from the shower he had taken, was plastered back against his skull. Anna studied him objectively. If they were together, really, would she feel a need to tell him that he needed a haircut? Would it bother her that he had on his sunglasses, even though it was getting dark outside? In the shower, he had sung something so badly out of key that she couldn't recognize it; she realized he was tone-deaf, and *that,* in some way, was endearing. She stared down at the wedding ring on his hand. He watched her and slowly eased his hand into his pocket.

"Does that make it disappear?" she asked him.

"I'm wearing it in case I get hit by a car or something," he explained sheepishly. "So that when Yvonne comes to identify the body, it'll be there on my hand."

"Where does she think you are right now, anyhow?" she asked him, realizing that he had no desire to pretend he wasn't married.

"Well, yeah," he said slowly, "There's that. I guess you're right. But all that's in my other life." He pulled her toward him for a brief kiss. The elevator door slid open and as Anna stepped out, she caught a glimpse of his dangerous, seductive smile in its polished brass reflection.

In Antoine's, Michael sucked his crawfish heads with relish and laid their carcasses on his plate. Anna suddenly realized she could not deny that there were things about him she found revolting. The waiter standing beside their table bowed discreetly and whisked away their plates. A silence fell between them. There were so many things they could not discuss. They'd never had such a long expanse of time together; all they'd ever had before was three or four quick hours in the lounge of some Ramada Inn in Houston. Anna would go to Neiman-Marcus before she met him and try on clothes for hours, almost in a trance, walking out to her car with bags of lingerie and spandex—tiny floraled minidresses, the kinds of things Van would disapprove of if he ever saw. She kept them hidden in a suitcase shoved underneath their bed. Michael seemed to like them fine.

"No one looks as good as you," he would say, when he slid into the booth beside her at whatever bar they had appointed as their meeting place. Maybe that was what kept her. But she knew there was more to it than that: the liquor in the drinks she ordered while she waited for him tasted sharp and acrid, her arms seemed tanner somehow, in the dim light of the Embers Lounge. When she drove I-10 to meet him, the wind from the air vent blew her hair up around her face, and once, right at dusk, the streetlamps on each side of a street had come on, one after another, stretching forward in a row in front of her. She felt wide awake and coiled tight, everything within her waiting for the minute when he would pull the room key out of his pocket and put it on the table with a click.

Michael threw his napkin on the table. "Do you . . ."

"What time is it?" she asked him at the same time.

"Let's go dancing," he said. She nodded.

"All right," she said briskly. Walking out of the restaurant, he took her arm.

They walked arm-in-arm down Bourbon Street, past the crowd staring up into the plate-glass window where a doughy, tired dancer stood, pouting in her black underwear, beckoning businessmen inside. Past a loose-limbed man managing a shell game on the corner, heckling a nervous audience toward him. Past the wild-eyed man who rushed through an open doorway and threw up, heaving, in the gutter. Anna clutched her purse. In the hotel room, the idea of New Orleans had been exciting, but now it seemed almost too feverish and loud.

"Where is it we're going?" she asked.

"Oh," Michael said authoritatively, "down Bourbon Street a-ways. The dance clubs in the gay section are much better."

After they passed a certain cross-street, they left most of the tourists behind. The crowds thinned out, and the men they passed were muscular; mostly edgy boys, leaning lazily up against the buildings. They had left the sound of Dixieland behind; there was nothing but the sullen throb of bass and drums, a litter of empty plastic cups heaped up in the gutters.

Inside the club, Anna was relieved to see other women. A strobe light pulsed from the corner; some sort of machine spit out a yellow fog that hovered above the floor. She walked toward the bar.

"Not here," Michael explained, grabbing her by the elbow. "This is the pickup bar. Upstairs is the dancing." Anna wondered how he knew—had he brought someone else to New Orleans for the weekend? Was it the kind of place where he would take his wife? Anna had never asked him about anything; there was no way she could know.

Upstairs, the burning fog was even thicker. Strobe lights flashed from all four walls, a mirrored ball dangled from the ceiling. The music was so loud Michael had to shout directly in her ear to ask her what she wanted from the bar.

"A gin and tonic," she said faintly.

"Let's dance," he suggested to her when he came back. He set her drink in a window sill. He led her out onto the dance floor and flailed his arms and legs happily. Anna rocked from one foot to the other. The music pulsed on and on, insistent and monotonous. The song lasted for at least fifteen minutes.

Sweet Marie's was a bar in Houston that Van had gone to when he was a bachelor. By the time he met Anna, he preferred quieter, higher-toned places; he only took her to Sweet Marie's once or twice. But she had been taken with the sign that rotated slowly on the building's flat roof: on one side, a female face was outlined with neon. The hair was yellow, the eyes round blue eggs which gave the face an expression of perpetual surprise. The sign was made so that the neon outlining the lips widened and puckered, as if the neon girl told every pickup truck that drove out of the parking lot a secret: "Y'all come back now" or "Don't be a stranger." Or maybe all it was, was that the girl on the sign was waiting, her face pretty and vacant, her eyes as round as eggs, with lipstick on her lips and makeup brushed around her eyes.

At Sweet Marie's, the house band played on Saturdays. The parking lot was always full. A waitress in a tight T-shirt walked around from behind the bar and tossed heavy handfuls of sawdust onto the floor. There were autographed photographs of Willie Nelson on the walls; pickled eggs that hovered, ghostly, in a jar beside the cash register.

Sweet Marie's mostly drew an older clientele: stringy, shovel-faced men, their mouths somber above their ties, their wives with stiffened, domelike hairdos and flashy diamond jewelry, years of smoking cigarettes the cause of the network of wrinkles in the corners of their mouths and eyes. Anna always felt out of place. She did not belong.

But once the music started, she forgot to feel uncomfortable, sat at a table staring at the whirling couples, the slick, fluid grace of a long-practiced step, the subtle give and take she doubted that she'd ever master. She wasn't even sure of the names of the steps. Van had tried to teach her, patiently, in their living room, but she had remained clumsy. When she'd been in high school, the dances had been called

the Latin Hustle and the Bus Stop. Later on, in college, when she had
gone out with her girlfriends to fashionable dance clubs, she didn't
even have to know how to dance to be considered a good partner. All
you did was move your shoulders and besides, you weren't really
dancing with anyone, even if there was a guy beside you.

This kind of dancing, the steps that wore Sweet Marie's floor-
boards down, it was like a foreign language. They took a certain
amount of skill, some silent communication she and Van just didn't
seem to have. Watching the dance floor, she felt a sturdy longing rise
up in her. Was it simply long, hard years together that gave these re-
signed couples their thoughtless grace? If she let go, if she and Van
weathered a lifetime together, would they know each other then? Or
was it just that she had ended up with the wrong man? Was it that
somewhere out there, there was someone else, and if she found him
they'd be smooth and easy together? Anna didn't know. It seemed to
her that there was a big valley between what you wanted and what
you got, a deep rift between what you dreamed of and what you set-
tled for.

"What are you thinking?" Michael leaned close and shouted in
her ear. Anna stared at the frantic dance floor. Underneath the
strobe lights, everyone looked different. Glamorous. Their faces
frozen in seductive expressions, then masked by darkness. Underneath the strobe lights, she noticed, even if they were standing
still, it looked like they had not stopped dancing.

"I think I'm ready to go now," she said to Michael suddenly.
"I'm too old for this." They navigated their way back down the
stairs.

"Not *you*," Michael exclaimed, grabbing her by the arm when
they got out to the street to steer her around the beer cups people
were tossing down from a balcony above them. "Not *you*."

"I *might* be too old," she said severely, giving him a kind of
warning.

In the hotel elevator they stood and stared at each other's reflections in the mirrored walls. Suddenly, Michael reached for her, putting his hands firmly behind her head and pulling her toward him.

"I love you," he said dramatically, beginning to kiss her. Anna felt an echo of his words rising to her lips. It would be so easy to whisper the phrase, to pretend it was true. A relief, the words as strong and illicit as a substance. She folded her lips together and turned her head away. She suddenly felt tired. *Really*, she reminded herself, half the time when someone says they love you, it's really just that they *want* you. Want to love you. She couldn't even fault Michael for the words he'd blurted out—she'd almost made the same mistake. She looked over at him and knew that in the second she'd refrained from speaking, something suddenly had ended, severed sharply, as defining as the click the motel room keys had made against the tables they'd leaned over, the nights they'd spent before, in Houston.

In the morning, her plane went first. She left him sitting wearily at the gate when her flight was called. He held his head like he had a hangover. It wasn't until she had boarded the plane and it was wheeling down the runway that she remembered she had left her ridiculous flower-covered hat on the chair beside him. She doubted he would mail it back—how could he explain arriving home with it to his wife? She settled in her seat, leaning her head back against the cushion, closing her eyes. Remembering his intent voice, the pressure of his hands arching her neck back, the sultry, humid smell of the city all around them. In the cab on their way to the airport, they had only spoken of things that slid past the dirty window, the cornice of a building, a wrought-iron fence, the muddy river.

With distance, Anna thought, even the most definite movement could become blurred. She realized that in a while—how long? a week? a month?—even her memory of New Orleans would lose its urgency. Already she was unsure she really knew the color of Michael's eyes. She stared out over the wing, Lake Ponchartrain spread out underneath. They must be blue, she told herself. You can't have forgotten to notice that. As blue as the shimmering lake below.

She realized she'd received more pleasure from the hat she'd purchased than she had from anything that had happened during the remainder of the weekend—that when she stepped off a curb on Decatur Street and, as a sudden gust of air swept across the street, held the hat on with one hand, she had been completely happy. In that moment, the smell of the river had blown toward her and New Orleans seemed slightly dangerous. It had given her a sense of satisfaction to realize no one knew exactly where she was.

Longing, sharp and deep and clear, suddenly cut through her. She swallowed, hard, fighting a scratchy feeling in the back of her throat. It looked as though the only souvenir she would have of New Orleans would be a sore throat. It suddenly ached with words she should have said—to Michael, just now, before the plane took off; Van, before she married him, five years before. Maybe something she should have told herself. She leaned her hot forehead against the cool plastic of the window, closing her eyes against the glare of the clouds. They were too far up for any sight of land. She felt flushed and hot and breathless—at one time she would have convinced herself that she was sick with something—love, Michael—but now she realized it was such a little thing: that momentary fever.

Deadman's Float

*P*aula said the lake was haunted, and she'd been at camp since the summer started. Her corner of the tent looked more like the inside of someone's bedroom than it did the corner of a moldy-smelling tent off in the woods somewhere. She had boxes of M&M's hidden underneath the uniforms inside her suitcase and pictures torn from *Tiger Beat* Scotch-taped to the wall above her cot. When she started talking about the ghost, she looked at Leah because Leah was the one who'd mentioned she heard things at night.

"There's a girl who paddles across the lake nights when the moon is absolutely, completely full," Paula swore. It was early in the morning, before breakfast, and they were getting ready for the flag ceremony. Paula had remembered about the ghost because the girl's initials were carved into the Tent Four platform. She yanked her suitcase out from underneath her cot to prove it. The initials J.L.P. were gouged into the wood underneath.

"Her name was Juliette Lynn Parsons," Paula explained. She told them the girl was always dressed in white and she had drowned a long time ago. There wasn't a single ripple in the water after her canoe went past. If you saw her, it meant you would probably drown within a day or two.

Cordele looked over Paula's shoulder. She put her fingers on the letters. "Those look pretty new," she interrupted. "And anyhow, wouldn't she be going around in her Girl Scout uniform if she drowned here?" She poked a finger at Paula's green bermuda shorts. Paula slid the suitcase back under her cot and looked at Cordele as if it were all completely obvious, and Cordele was just too dumb to see it.

"I don't believe in ghosts, anyhow," Katie told them suddenly. "My mom says things like that are just the product of an overactive imagination." She touched her badge sash and yawned. "Is it straight?" she questioned Leah. She pirouetted in a circle.

Leah was impressed by Katie because during the year, Katie had explained to them, she took ballet. Her family had a boat on Lake Lanier. She knew how to waterski. She looked like something from the Girl Scout catalog, with her beret tilted over her hair and the badge sash covered with embroidered disks flung across one shoulder.

"It's straight," Leah told her. She put her own sash on. It was limp and wrinkled because it wasn't new like Katie's, it was from the secondhand store. Her Girl Scout Trefoil and the pin she had gotten at the Juliette Low Birthplace the time she and her mother went to Savannah were almost the only things on it. "What about mine?" she asked, but she didn't look at Katie, she looked down at the floor. Cordele was sitting on the wooden rail outside the tent, and Leah could see Paula standing on the path, kicking rocks toward the tents further down the trail. Katie brushed her hair. She barely looked at Leah.

"Yeah," she said. "It's fine."

Back in the winter, Leah had tried to get the Housekeeping badge, which was on page 143 of the *Girl Scout Handbook*. She picked it because it was something Mrs. Fulton, the troop leader, had suggested. Housekeeping was not like Horsemanship or Water Sports. You could do it at home. It involved cleaning house and cooking meals. *Things every girl should know,* Mrs. Fulton told her brightly, after the third badge ceremony when everyone but Leah received a small white envelope with at least one badge in it. Leah's mother thought Housekeeping was a fine idea—she had just taped a chart she'd made to the front of the refrigerator showing the different days she wanted Leah and J.D. to cook supper. The chart was big, done in black Magic Marker. It also listed the days Leah should do laundry and when J.D. was supposed to work outside and mow the grass.

That chart was something the family counselor had suggested, the one time they had gone to see him. The family counselor had been a man with a large adam's apple that bobbed slowly when he talked. When they walked into his office, J.D. chose the chair farthest away from him. He slouched into his jacket and stared at the sign on the counselor's desk that said NO SMOKING PLEASE. J.D. was *the identified patient* in the family, the counselor explained after a while. He was not really the problem. J.D. looked around the room and fumbled in his jacket pocket. He slowly lit a cigarette.

"Look at him," their mother said. "You mean to tell me *he* is not a problem?" J.D. flicked ash onto the floor. The counselor's face slowly turned red. Leah noticed that even the tops of his ears were pink. She folded her knees up underneath her and moved around in her chair so she could see the street outside the window. A green car passed, and then a white one, and then a dirty, yellow pickup truck.

"Son," the counselor said, "would you mind putting that out?"

J.D. looked at the hot tip of the cigarette. He held it up and studied it.

"Fuck you," he told the counselor. He raised the cigarette up to his lips.

Leah had been very excited about the Housekeeping badge at first. It was a tiny milk bottle and an egg embroidered onto a blue background the color of the sky. Leah looked at her mother's *International Cookbook* before her nights to cook. She burned things in the bottoms of all the pans, trying to make strawberry crepes while her mother was in her bedroom with the lights off, resting after work.

"What is this shit?" J.D. said the first time Leah cooked, when she put the flabby, burnt-up ovals that were supposed to be crepes on his plate. J.D. still came home for supper then.

"It's food," their mother said. "Your sister worked very hard. You had better eat it." J.D. threw his napkin down. His eyes were glassy.

"We don't have a good crepe pan," Leah tried to explain to him. "That's why they stuck. But it's a real good recipe."

J.D. stood up and turned his back. "I'm going down to Dave's," he said. Dave's was the pizza place down at the corner. "I don't have to eat this crap."

For Leah to get the Housekeeping badge, they had to have family meetings once a month. "Maybe if we take votes on everything," she coaxed her mother, "J.D. will feel better." But when it was time for the first meeting J.D. refused to leave his room.

"I don't have the time for any of this dumb-ass Girl Scout shit," he said when she went up to his room to tell him they were waiting for him. He was lying on his bed with his Dingo boots planted against the wall and screechy music on his record player. He looked at Leah and dragged his feet down. A long black mark scratched across the paint.

On the chart taped to the refrigerator, it said J.D. would cook dinner twice a week. But he only did it once, and that time he didn't really cook because he came home with a pizza he had gotten at Dave's.

"Where are you getting the money to pay for this?" their mother asked. J.D. didn't answer.

"How much money do you have, James?" Her voice was quiet. They were standing in the kitchen and Leah was putting plates onto the table. She laid the silverware beside the napkins she had tried to pull into graceful shapes like swans. Their mother walked toward J.D. He gazed wildly over her shoulder.

"If this is a campaign to get me to send you to your father," she said suddenly, "*he* doesn't want you either."

J.D. looked at her and then he turned toward the sink and reached up to the magnetic knife holder hung above it. He yanked a knife down off it. It made a slippery noise when it slid across the magnet. He looked at her. His face was strained. He tossed the knife from one hand to the other. He was six foot two already.

"Why couldn't it be *you* who went away?" he screamed. That was the first night the police came.

J.D. told Leah he had *friends*. He had places he could go. It wasn't like he even *wanted* to be in their stupid white-bread house in their stupid neighborhood where their neighbors were always doing stupid things, like mowing their grass and playing their pianos and listening behind their doors so they could call the police the first minute they heard something. He didn't talk at all to their mother. He just came in late at night and went out early in the morning. It had been fall when their father left. It was winter when J.D. quit coming home from school until after it got dark. He'd throw his books down on the chair beside the living room door and stomp up to his room. His door would slam and Leah could hear the sound of one of his records on the turntable.

In the afternoons, when Leah was on the bus coming home from the middle school, she'd look out the window when it went down Warner Street, and that was where he'd be. Always with a bunch of other boys, their hands stuck deep into the pockets of their jackets, their shoulders hunched. They were always walking toward downtown, even though the high school didn't let out until three forty-five.

"Your brother looks like Jesus." People at school came up to Leah in the halls to tell her so. "He looks like John Lennon." And then they'd look at her. "Why does he act like *that*?" they'd ask. "Why is his hair so long?" *Their* older brothers were on the football team, *their* older sisters were cheerleaders. *They* said J.D. wasn't anything, besides a freak. He wore little wire-framed sunglasses, even inside school. Sometimes, when Leah saw him on the street, he looked like he was blind.

"I've been coming to Camp Columbus since *second grade*," Katie told them when they were walking to the flag ceremony, "and I've never, ever, seen anything that looked like it could be a ghost." Paula walked ahead of them, acting like she didn't care what they were saying. Her white uniform blouse gaped open in between the buttons, but she didn't seem to notice.

Leah didn't say anything to Katie although there *was* a bird off toward the lake that cried, at night. It was the only one. And every night the watchman marched up and down the trail, shining his flashlight underneath the tent platforms as he went by. Leah didn't know what he was looking for. "Tent Four," he always said. "You girls okay?" Then he was past their tent and they could hear his feet crunching through the leaves on the path. "Tent Five?" he'd say above the crickets, and it would be a second before Paula started talking again, telling some story about what-all it was that she had done in Columbus, with her flashlight in her lap, pointed upward at her chin so that it made her look like she had awful holes where her mouth and eyes should be.

Back in the winter, Leah's mother had said *their* house was haunted, but she was talking about a different kind of ghost—

sometimes it seemed like Leah's father was still there. Still walking around. Sometimes Leah thought she could hear him slamming the front door, early in the morning before it was even light, going out to get the paper lying in the driveway. Sometimes at night, she thought she heard him in the kitchen, when she woke up and the kitchen light was falling through the doorway against the rug in the hall. But usually it was J.D., and once it was their mother. When Leah went in to see, she was at the kitchen table in her nightgown, and there was a single beer on the tabletop in front of her. Mascara was smudged around her eyes.

"Are you waiting up for J.D.?" Leah had asked.

Her mother looked right at her, but she didn't say anything. Leah went back to her bedroom and tried to think of something so that she would go to sleep. *Just think black,* her mother used to say when she was little. *Just think black and then you'll fall asleep.* But thinking black was like thinking about being dead. It made Leah think of the two cats they'd had that had gotten hit by cars and were buried in the backyard. The window above her bed opened up onto the dark backyard. Cold air slid around the edges of the glass. There was the sound of the kitchen light being turned off, and later, when Leah had finally almost gone to sleep, there was a bumping noise upstairs, like J.D. had finally come home and was taking off his boots.

If they dropped the flag down in the dirt, they were supposed to burn it.

"So what," Paula said. They were walking to the ragged, half-mowed clearing in the trees with the flagpole in the middle of it, where everyone was waiting for the flag ceremony to start. The night before, Paula and Leah had been the color guard, which meant they were the ones who took the flag down before it got dark. When they unhooked it from the chain, Paula had let her end droop into the dirt. Leah hadn't said anything.

Today, Leah was the one who was the flag bearer. She carried the triangle that was the folded flag carefully in her hands. She made sure the stars were facing *up*, the point of the triangle was facing *forward*. She marched toward the clearing. Cordele and Paula were the color guard behind her; Katie behind them.

"Leah's walking like she thinks she's in the army," Paula observed, and Leah was embarrassed. She had just been thinking about something else. She stopped lifting her feet so high off the ground and let them shuffle through the dirt.

She stopped abruptly in front of the flagpole and then turned around. Katie and Cordele and Paula whirled around behind her. They stared out at everybody else, standing in a horseshoe shape in front of them. "Attention," Katie shrieked. She was the only one who knew all of the flag ceremony's words, so she was always the commander. The second-graders' end of the horseshoe was ragged. Most of the counselors were at that end. Some of the little girls didn't have complete uniforms. They wore their badge sashes over the muddy-green tie-dyed shirts they'd made in Crafts. Most of the Brownies' uniforms were a mouse-colored sort of brown. They looked like they'd been wadded up in suitcases. Katie started the Girl Scout oath. Leah stared at the ragged line of pines around the edges of the clearing. They looked like fingers pointing toward the sky. She looked down at the ground, at the tiny flat sheets of mica that winked back at her. Katie poked her in the back. There was a solemn hush. She and Cordele and Katie started unfolding the flag. Everyone was quiet while they hooked it to the chain and raised it up. There wasn't any wind. The flag hung there like a piece of laundry and everybody just looked at it for a minute.

"They treat us like slaves," Paula announced. It was after breakfast and they had just checked the list tacked up outside the dining hall to see what chores they had. They had latrine duty again, which meant they had to scrub the toilets in the bathhouse. Every morning, the counselors made up a roster—every tent was supposed to have a different duty. The Brownies were not very good at cleaning toilets. Katie and Cordele and Paula and Leah—Tent Four—were the oldest girls. They almost always had latrine duty.

"I don't know why we even look at that piece of paper," Paula said. "We already *know* what it is we have to do." Earlier, she had pointed out the fact that the counselors never gave themselves any of the chores. The counselors had it way too easy, Paula said. They had their own tent, up next to the dining hall. It even had electricity. When Tent Four woke up in the mornings, they could hear the radio the counselors had up there, playing "Muskrat Love" or "Goodbye, Yellow Brick Road." The sound was loud, slipping down toward the lake from between the trees.

"Why did you even come here?" Cordele asked Paula abruptly. She was down on her knees scrubbing at the toilet. She looked up. Her face was red. "If it's so awful, why don't you just *leave?*" Paula looked at her. Her mouth was open. She turned her head and looked out through the door toward the lake. Then she turned back around and put her hands on her hips.

"I could go anywhere," she told them. "I could have gone to Six Flags if I wanted."

Cordele flushed the toilet. She stood up. "I think you're here because there's nobody that wants you."

"You're just jealous," Paula said. She cleared her throat. "My sister's coming to see me today," she said. "While you-all are at Swimming. She's going to take me out to eat. Maybe to McDonald's. I was going to try to bring you something, but I don't guess I really can."

The first day of Leah's camp session, the bus her mother put her on had jerked to a stop in Columbus, where Leah waited patiently underneath a drooping paper banner with CAMP COLUMBUS written on it for the counselors to drive up with the camp van. The inside of the bus station stank like exhaust, which always made her feel like she was getting carsick.

Two counselors came to pick her up. They both were very tan. They kept leaning over the front seat to look back at her. She was the only person waiting underneath the sagging banner. "Most people's parents drive them to the camp," one of the counselors told her. The other counselor turned the radio up, and Leah just looked out the window at the telephone pole–straight pine trees flashing past them and the patches of blood-colored dirt.

At Camp Columbus, there was a dock down by the water, and a twisted nylon rope hung down with aqua and white floats that marked off the little beach beside it. Up the hill where the counselor had parked the van, there was the bathhouse and the dining hall and the huge charred-up fire ring where they all sang, "Make new friends but keep the old" at the end of every one-week session, when the girls who were leaving cried and the ones who were staying through the summer acted like they didn't care at all, that leaving was a bad thing and not what almost everybody wanted.

The tents curved in a wiggly arc around one end of the lake. In the daylight, Leah could see them through the trees, bright yellow through the blackberries and poison ivy. At night, before it got too late, she would stand outside Tent Four, and if she squinted hard enough, she could see the light from someone's flashlight glowing against the yellow canvas of one of the other tents or bobbing through the trees along the path that led up to the bathroom. She could never hear what was going on in the other tents, but it was good, she thought, to know that they were there. At night, right after the campfire, when they came back down the hill to go to bed, the watchman was always sitting on the dock eating his lunch. Sometimes Leah could smell his cigarettes and see their red glow when he threw them toward the water. They reminded her of her father and the way, before he left, sometimes he sat on the back steps of the house at night and smoked, one cigarette after the other, staring out at the backyard. Leah watched him through her open bedroom window. He held himself very still. Leah's eyes would start to close and finally she would lie down on the bed and fall asleep.

The first night Leah was at Camp Columbus, Katie had sworn there had never been a watchman at Camp Columbus before, but that year they had three.

"It's to keep the boys out," Paula said. They were lying in their sleeping bags on their cots. Paula and Katie had gotten the best ones because they'd been at Camp Columbus since the very beginning of the summer—they had gotten to switch cots after the two girls who had been there for the first three sessions left.

"They don't want us to have any sort of social contact whatsoever," Paula explained to Cordele and Leah, who were new. She paused. "Although there's a cute boy who washes dishes at the dining hall. He looks like Scott Baio."

"Yuck," Cordele commented.

Paula ignored her. "He's probably going to ask me out," she told them.

None of them wanted to go to sleep. Leah felt strange, lying in a sleeping bag out in the middle of the woods with these three girls she didn't even know. The sleeping bag she'd brought had been J.D.'s; it even smelled like him, like cigarettes and the incense he was always burning in his room, although Leah wasn't sure when he'd last slept in it. He didn't care much about the woods anymore.

"I"m sure he won't mind if you take it," their mother had told her. In May, J.D. had gotten caught taking money out of the cash register at his job, and now he was out at Beaverdam, the juvenile detention center. Leah hadn't seen him since the summer started. The inside of his sleeping bag was soft red flannel printed with a pattern of flying ducks and Irish setters. J.D. had had his sleeping bag a long time, since back when he and Leah had played like they were camping in the backyard, and that had been when Leah was a Brownie and he was a Webelo. The next year after that might have been the year he decided things like Boy Scouts were stupid.

That first night, Katie and Paula had their flashlights on. Katie sat cross-legged on her cot, picking through a box of candy her mother had sent from home, holding pieces up to her flashlight to see if she could tell if they were creams or toffees. Outside, the night watchman's boots scraped on the gravel of the path. His footsteps stopped outside the tent. "'Tent Four?" he said. His voice slid in between the tent flaps. "Everything okay?"

Paula stopped talking. Leah could hear the chink of his keys when he walked past.

"Do you-all know?" she said after a minute. She lowered her voice and looked around like she was checking to make sure they all were listening. "Do you-all know what a *blow-job* is?"

"Yeah, sure," Cordele said. "Of course. Big deal." Her voice was edgy.

Leah was quiet.

"Like going to third base?" Katie asked. She didn't seem that interested.

"What do *you* think, Leah?" Paula asked. Leah didn't say anything.

"Of course *Leah* doesn't know," Paula answered herself. "Because she's such a baby." She pointed her flashlight at each one of them in turn.

"This is what it is," she told them. "You take his *thing* and do like this."

"You mean you put it in your *mouth*?" Leah said it before she even thought. She looked around. Paula lowered her flashlight from her face.

"It's true," she said.

Cordele's face was disgusted. "Nuh-uh," she said. "That's gross."

Even Katie seemed surprised. "How do you know?" she said. "My mother never told me *that*."

"My brother-in-law told me." Paula looked at them smugly. They'd already heard all about Paula's sister and her husband and the little baby her sister had. How Paula lived with them instead of with her mother. How Paula's brother-in-law was a *hunk*, cuter even than Shaun Cassidy. He drove a bright red Thunderbird. "T-bird," Paula said importantly. It was one of the first things she had told them. Her brother-in-law took her to Baskin-Robbins for ice cream while her sister was at home with the baby. "My sister used to be a fox," Paula had explained, "but after the baby she got kind of blubbery." She cocked her head as if she was listening to something someone else was saying. Her sister, she said firmly, was a drag.

She ran her flashlight beam over the canvas of the tent. Everyone was quiet. "You're making that up," Cordele said finally. Leah slid down in her sleeping bag and put her pillow over her ears.

In March, Leah's mother had started bringing home brochures for places she called *luxury communities*. Luxury communities were all on the east side of town. They had recreation rooms and swimming pools and saunas and shag carpeting.

"We're just two little old peas in a great big pod, aren't we, Leah-Bird?" her mother said. Her mother hadn't called her Leah-Bird since she was little, and Leah didn't think that they should move because someday J.D. would be coming back. He wasn't always going to live in the little apartment their father had driven over from Birmingham to help him find the month before. He wasn't always going to work at Long John Silver's, which was the only place he could find a job where they wouldn't make him get a haircut.

Her mother sat at the dining room table with a pen and the brochures spread out around her.

"This one has a recreation center," she said. "Leah, honey, how'd you like to live in *this?*" Her pen tapped against a photograph of a row of brick buildings flanked by a kidney-bean shaped pool. Leah liked the room she had, the way she'd gotten to pick out the frilly curtains and help paint all the dresser drawers. She didn't want to have to move and start going to the other middle school where there were lots of rednecks and everyone dressed bad and lived way out somewhere in the country.

"Who cares?" she said, under her breath. "Who cares?" But all her mother said was *What, honey?* She picked up a pen and drew a careful circle around a phone number on one of the brochures.

"I'll call them in the morning," she told Leah.

The part of the day at Camp Columbus Leah hated most was Swimming, which came an hour after lunch. She hated Swimming more than anything else they did because before it they had to change into their swimsuits in front of one another. In the mornings, when they first got up, it was easy for her to get dressed huddled down inside her sleeping bag. She just pretended she was cold. But in the middle of the afternoon it wasn't like she could just jump back into her sleeping bag. And Paula always noticed if she turned her back. Paula would look at Leah's itchy training bra and say, *So where did you get that? K-Mart?* Paula's bras looked like the kind Leah's mother wore. She left them lying on her cot, right there in plain view. Cordele swore to Leah that Paula *wanted* them to see them. Paula claimed that at her school in Columbus, her nickname was Boom-Boom. If they wanted, she said, looking at them, they were free to call her that. She tossed back her hair and stuck out her chest.

Leah tried to get her swimsuit on without taking her T-shirt all the way off. It was getting all stretched out, from the way she yanked it up over her shoulders. Paula sat on her cot, stuffing things into her knapsack. It was, she told them airily, her time of the month—she had gotten special permission to miss Swimming. Her sister was driving out from Columbus to visit, to take her out to dinner at the McDonald's on the interstate.

"You're going to miss the certification," Cordele told her. Paula shrugged her shoulders.

"I got permission to go," she said in a loud voice. "My sister's taking me out to dinner and then we'll go out to a movie. At my sister's, I can do whatever I feel like. We'll have potato chips, and Cokes, whatever."

"Would you sneak something back?" Katie asked her.

"Maybe," Paula said, but then she looked at Cordele. "I don't know," she said.

"If you're gone today," Leah reminded her, "you can't get your junior lifesaving certificate. Then you can't be a lifeguard."

"Who wants to be a lifeguard?" Paula said. She shoved a hot-pink pair of sunglasses into her bag. "I sure don't. You dummies are brainwashed."

The bottom of the lake was slimy reddish clay. From the very first day, Leah had hated the way it squished underneath her feet when she tried to touch bottom.

"Okay," Melissa, the swimming counselor, told them. She held a clipboard and a piece of paper out in front of her. A whistle dangled around her neck, hanging from a chain. Melissa's face was red and the skin on her nose was peeling. She squinted. Leah and Cordele and Katie were lined up on the dock in front of her. The littler girls, the Brownies, were running up and down the beach behind them, singing something stupid. It sounded like "Little Bunny Foo-foo," a song they all had to sing at the sing-alongs after dinner, around the campfire. "Little Bunny Foo-foo" was such a retarded song, the second-graders loved it. After the first night, Leah and Cordele had quit even moving their lips.

"Okay," Melissa said. "Today we're doing the test to see if y'all can get your junior lifesaving certification." She looked down at her piece of paper. "Today we'll do the water part. Tomorrow I'll test you on the lifesaving, the mouth-to-mouth."

"Gross," Cordele said and made a kissing sound. Melissa stood in front of them with her hands on her hips.

"Today, what we're going to do is this," she continued firmly. "First, you're going to tread water in your clothes for five minutes. A shirt and a pair of pants. With your swimsuit underneath. When I blow the whistle, you'll throw your clothes up on the dock and swim across the lake. You can use any stroke you want, except dog-paddle. I'll be right behind in the canoe."

"This is retarded," Cordele said. "Why do we have to do it?"

"Because this is junior lifesaving. What would happen if you fell off a boat? You have to be able to swim in your clothes. They're heavier." Melissa looked at them severely. "You girls are *Girl Scouts*, remember? The little girls are watching. You-all are the oldest." She paused and wrinkled up her nose. "You're supposed to be the best." Leah looked at Cordele and Katie. They both looked bored.

"I *can't* do this," she whispered suddenly. Katie shrugged and moved away from her, lining up her feet at the edge of the dock so that when Melissa blew the whistle she could make a perfect dive.

Their clothes *were* heavier. Although Katie and Cordele didn't seem to notice. They bobbed up and down in the water solemnly, and behind them, Leah could see the aqua and white weights that cordoned off the shallow water. Leah's pants dragged against her legs like they were coated with cement. The water was warm, and it had started going up her nose. She flailed her arms and bicycled her legs. No one said anything. There was just the sound of churning water and the little girls giggling and splashing in the shallow water. Melissa stood on the dock, looking at her stopwatch.

"How long?" Leah gasped, trying to tilt her head up so that she could see her.

Melissa was silent. She stared at the stopwatch. "One minute," she intoned.

Leah's arms and legs felt heavy. They sliced slowly through the water, as if it were a wind pushing against her, bending her bones back. It was harder and harder to keep her head above the water. The lake was dark and smelled like mud. It was impossible to see the bottom. Melissa had said that at its deepest, the lake was only ten feet deep. Leah's legs churned slowly. She squinted, staring down through the water, but all she saw was the flash of her own legs. Like silver, darting fish. It didn't even seem that they belonged to her. The dark water gaped. No matter how far Leah sank, her toes would never touch the bottom.

"How long now?" she shrieked, spitting out the water that had gotten in her mouth.

"Three minutes," Melissa said and yawned.

Leah's legs felt like they were made of wood. She looked across the water at Cordele. Her face was expressionless. She methodically moved her legs up and down.

"Okay," Melissa said finally. "Throw your clothes up here."

Leah struggled with her Camp Columbus T-shirt. It was soggy and stretched out and she realized that when she tried to pull it over her head, she would be completely underwater, unable to move her arms. She wondered how far she would sink before she pulled it off. The T-shirt felt like gauze, and her hands were tangled in it. She yanked it over her head and slung it toward the dock. Katie and Cordele had already started swimming. Melissa was in the canoe, holding her paddle across her legs, looking back at Leah.

"You can swim faster than that, Leah," she shouted.

Leah started with the backstroke because she didn't want to put her face into the water. She lay against the surface of the water and the blue sky and the pine trees jerked in front of her while she tried to catch her breath. She hadn't ever been very good at the backstroke and her arms felt like someone had pulled at them, the way when she was little, she and J.D. pulled at wishbones until they cracked. She kept stopping to tread water so she could see how far off course she had gotten. Katie and Cordele were far in front of her, Melissa in the canoe a few feet ahead.

"You'll never finish," Melissa finally shouted to her, "if you keep with the back stroke. You need to do the crawl."

Leah turned over and lowered her face into the water. When she tilted it to get air, she caught a glimpse of sky and shore and dirty water. Her breath was ragged.

Every swimming lesson since Leah had started camp, Melissa had taught them something. First it was mouth-to-mouth, how to do it on a baby or a grown-up. How to brace your body on the shore and pull someone who was floundering and panicked in. Different ways to float. Melissa told them stories about people who had waited in the water for hours before anyone could get to them. One of the ways to rest while you were waiting was the deadman's float. Leah thought of something white and heavy floating in some scummy water like a log. The deadman's float was perfect if you were out on a boat that started sinking and you were waiting to be rescued.

They'd never had to do the deadman's float, really. It was just something it was good to know about, in case of an emergency. All they had to do was lie face down in the water with their arms stretched out, then turn their heads barely to the side, for air.

Leah was treading water. She felt so tired. Katie and Cordele were almost at the opposite shore. She didn't think she could catch up with them. She didn't think that she could breathe. She remembered about the deadman's float. She stretched her arms up and put her face into the water. She couldn't float at all. Her legs pulled her downward. She was underwater; she could see the brownish, silty water. It was the color of tea; everything was quiet underneath it. Leah's hair waved back and forth in front of her face, like grass, like leaves, like there was a wind to move it.

Paula claimed you could even see the girl who drowned in daylight. Was she still drifting underwater, her hair moving like mud-colored seaweed? Paula had told them the girl was just their age; she had drowned the summer before she started seventh grade. The water seemed dark and warm and peaceful. Leah pushed herself back up to the surface.

"Please let me in the boat," she shouted to Melissa. "I can't go any farther."

"Nope," Melissa said. "You don't have far to go." Her voice was firm, the same way Coach Fredricks's would be during the year, at school, when Leah was running track in P.E., when the coach would yell, *It hurts so good* while someone threw up on the grass beside the bleachers.

"Let me in the boat," she said. She treaded water beside it.

"You can do it," Melissa said. She started paddling faster.

"I can't," Leah shouted. "I don't want to anymore. Please let me in," she begged. The water around her swirled in tiny perfect whirlpools where Melissa had just pushed her paddle through it. Leah could barely keep her head above the water enough to see that Melissa wasn't going to turn the canoe around and come back.

Paula got back after supper, after the campfire, after the rest of them had already straggled down the hill in the half-dark and gotten into their sleeping bags. Leah was so tired she could barely stay awake.

"I found out why there are security guards this year," Paula announced to them importantly as soon as she came in. She pulled on the Camp Columbus T-shirt and the shorts she slept in. She climbed into her sleeping bag.

"Why?" Katie asked.

"I don't know if I should say. My sister said I shouldn't even know." Paula's flashlight beam was turned toward the ceiling and she looked up at it coyly.

"What?" Cordele said. "You have to tell."

"It's this," she said. She lowered her voice to a whisper. "There's this man . . ."

It had been in all the papers. The Atlanta TV crews had been in Columbus—it had been on the news. They hadn't heard anything because they were at camp. Even though Columbus was so close. But everybody else knew. There was a curfew in Columbus.

The man had killed six women. He drove up and down the streets of Columbus, Paula said theatrically, in a beat-up Chevrolet. There had been a artist's drawing of what the police thought he looked like in the Columbus paper. That was what Paula had seen that made her ask her sister what it was all about.

Paula said the picture looked like Charles Manson, hair out around his face like *this*. She measured with her hands around her head. The man had little-bitty eyes, the way Charles Manson did in *Helter-Skelter*, which had been on TV the spring before. Leah had not been supposed to watch *Helter-Skelter*, but her mother had had a date that night and hadn't known.

"He wraps a panty hose around their necks," Paula told them. "He pulls tighter and tighter until they're dead. He climbs in through their bedroom windows."

Everyone was quiet. "He does something to them, after they're dead," Paula said. "My sister wouldn't tell me what. I think," she said slowly, "he does something with his thing, after they're dead."

"You're a liar," Leah screamed suddenly. She jumped off her cot. Her sleeping bag slid onto the floor. Her arms were flailing. She lunged toward Paula and started shaking her. "You think you know everything, but you really don't know nothing," she yelled. The watchman pulled the tent-flap back. His flashlight was so bright it hurt their eyes.

"What's all this?" he said. Leah pulled her sleeping bag up off the floor and straightened it on her cot.

"Just playing a game," Katie said after a minute.

"I'll send a counselor in here if I hear another thing," he said. He let the tent flap drop back down.

Paula turned her flashlight off. No one said anything.

"You're just *white trash.*" Cordele's voice was soft in the sudden darkness. "All you are is trash," she said to Paula.

"You cheerleader piece of shit," Paula said back. She paused. "You fucking baby," she hissed toward Leah's cot. None of them could believe the words that hung there in the air.

Leah woke up abruptly, not knowing where she was. It was dark, really dark, like her head was underneath her sleeping bag. Her heart beat hard. She was standing up.

"Cordele?" she whispered. "Paula? Are you there?" Her eyes were open wide.

She felt leaves underneath her feet. She could hear the creaking of tree limbs and the wind. There was a little light now, faint, from the sky, above the branches. Somehow, she was outside the tent beside the wooden platform. She put out her hand and touched it. She listened hard. She could hear the watchman, whistling. His flashlight beam played over the bushes.

The first time she'd walked in her sleep had been right after she and her mother moved into the new apartment. Her mother told her she'd been sitting in the living room when Leah walked out of her bedroom. She walked through the living room and out the unlocked door. Her mother had read that it was dangerous to wake someone who was sleepwalking so she just followed behind Leah, watching closely. Leah walked toward the swimming pool. Her eyes were open. Her mother said, *Leah?* But she kept on. Her mother was afraid she would drown. She shook her by the shoulder.

That was when Leah woke up. The swimming pool was a blue shimmery disk, curved in a shape like a pin her grandmother had worn once. The underwater lights were on. She could hear the cars down on the highway, going past.

"Where were you going?" her mother asked her. Leah didn't know. She didn't even know how she had gotten there. She was still half-asleep.

"Home," she told her mother.

It was cold; Leah heard the sound of the watchman's feet crunching on the path. She was just in the clothes she slept in, a white T-shirt and panties. The T-shirt was faded; it brushed against her thighs. She tried to yank it further down her legs. The watchman's feet got closer. She leapt up the two stairs to the tent and ducked inside.

She lay awake for a long time. She put out her hand and touched the thin canvas walls of the tent. She didn't feel any safer than she had waking up out in the dark, half-asleep, her bare feet on the ground. The watchman walked past again. He was whistling a song her mother used to sing. Leah could hear the jingle of his keys, the creak of the leather holster she knew he wore across one shoulder. There were goose-bumps on her arms and she pulled them under the sleeping bag. Katie turned over on the cot across from her. Out on the lake a bird made one sharp cry. Paula's pictures torn from magazines stared down from the walls. There was a splash, but Leah knew there was no way that it could be a person, not even someone drowning.

"Who's there?" the watchman called, and Leah held herself quiet in the rustling sleeping bag. Waiting for an answer, but she knew from hikes and woodcraft that the trees outside the tent were straight and leaned toward each other densely. Brambles spilled down into the deep ravines and vines of poison ivy, thick as snakes, twined up and down the trees. If there was someone out there, he wasn't going to answer. She pushed herself down into her sleeping bag. She heard the sound of Paula's sigh. Some nights, Paula talked in her sleep, but when they sat up in the dark and questioned her, she wouldn't say a thing. Paula had been the one who convinced Leah to lie down on the floor, the night they'd planned to have the seance. She vowed she knew a way that they could lift her, just with their fingertips. She held her index finger against Leah's side. Katie and Cordele stood at her head and feet. Paula said the magic word but nothing ever happened. Leah felt immovable as stone.

"Think about air," Katie had cried, and Leah closed her eyes. *Think black,* she had told herself. She wished she was asleep.

Eggs for Young America

Curtis

*T*oward the city limits sign, the chicken plant weights down the sky like a brick.

Before that, closer to town, are the sullen coils of the copper-colored river, the rusty coils leaching through the sodden bedsprings the transients drag into the heavy brush between the water and the railroad tracks.

At night, their fires gleam like eyes. In the mornings, Curtis clambers up the clay gullies, up the twisty streets, to rail and rest, to knock on doors and ask for water. His eyes are hard as hatchet heads. The cops, they all know him by name.

When he stands on the sagging, slanted porch of the white house on the corner, the skinny black-haired girl who comes to the door won't even open it completely. She scrabbles at the door to flick the latch when he puts his foot between it and the jamb. *God damn,* he tells her. His curses are fluid, rhythmic, dull. *God damn you.* She hunches her shoulders, trying to keep the black strap of the slip she's in from sliding down. *A lightning bolt will rain down on you,* he shouts. *On this house. This dirty street. Rain down on this entire-ly mis-be-gotten town.* She wrestles the door shut and peers through the dirty glass beside it, hoping that he'll turn his back, go down the walk and back to the street, the river, before she has to leave for work and unlock the front door.

The cops catch up with him on the Avenue, a corner and three Dempsey dumpsters later, after he's dug out an artificial orange plant, a broken Mister Coffee. A squad car and a motorcycle string behind him in a long parade. *CURTIS*, their police loudspeaker crackles. *PLEASE GET OUT OF THE STREET. CURTIS. IT'S NOT GOOD TO WALK IN THE MIDDLE OF THE STREET.*

He weaves his way over to the sidewalk. The motorcycle cop salutes him with his hand.

He carries his artificial orange plant, brandishing the oily, olive-colored branches that will never droop from lack of water. He heads down the street, toward his space beside the river. He already has a moldy chair he wrestled down the streets and through the gullies, his mattress, and now he has his plant. When it gets too cold, he'll leave them there and hop a train for somewhere else. A better climate. Florida. When he comes back in the spring, the river will have risen, fallen and risen again. Tattered plastic bags will be caught in the branches up above the dirty water line. The water moccasins will be nesting in the up-torn roots of the trees that line the edges of the river.

Nadine

The Hardigree house oversees the worn-out neighborhood like a giant, sinking ship. It lists sideways on its foundation; majestic, doomed, and frivolous as the Titanic. There used to be chandeliers in the wide front hall, now all there are, are twisted snaky wires. The Hardigree house has three full stories and a cupola on top with windows facing four directions, blank as eyes. A jigsawed, scrollworked porch wraps three-fourths of the way around it. The front steps are caved in. The mahogany banisters inside are scratched and splintered. The mantelpieces were torn out by vandals. A ROOMS FOR RENT sign leans sideways on the weedy lawn.

Everyone knows the Hardigree house: the cops, the historic preservationists who call the City Council to protest that even though it's falling down, the Chamber of Commerce ought to buy it. The Atlanta developer who'd love to get his fingers on the land—prime Jiffy-Stop real estate—calls the aged, senile owner and crosses his fingers, hoping one of the house's dirty tenants will set fire to it, arson. Out-of-town tourists pass it by—there's no historical marker out in front to inform them of the history of the first carpetbagging Hardigree whose mercantile fortune built it, back when all these streets, Park and Davis and the Avenue, were lined with gleaming, alabaster-sided Greek Revivial houses—houses set into their green lawns like diamonds with carbon-copy gazebos nestling in the corners. Behind the houses, the hills, littered with tarpaper shacks for the textile workers, sloped gently downward to the brackish river. Now the textile row is Black—the angular creosoted fingers of the railroad trestles cut across it. Most of the Avenue is razed. The houses left lie beached on the crests of the hills, the wreckage of their fine front yards around them.

But the front porch of the Hardigree house is still intact and that porch is where Nadine and her roommates live most of the year, on the sagging sofa. It's where they drag the kegs in summer when they have a party, where Lisa Marie dyed Nadine's hair jet-black and streaked it with blue Crazy Color—and that had really changed her. The porch is where they smoke their cigarettes and drink their jelly-glasses full of Tang and vodka, staring at the rush-hour traffic, watching all the regular people hunched behind the wheels of their late-model cars, the secretaries with their bleached-blonde, bouffant hair, the businessmen who loosen their ties and peer into their rearview mirrors. They don't look out their windows. Their eyes are fixed upon the cars in front, beside them. They are in a hurry to get to a better section of the city.

Jimbo

James Beauregard Durham the Third walks through his parents' house, which smells of lemon furniture polish and carelessly laid out bowls of potpourri. Once his parents' house overlooked a cow field. Now there's a wrought-iron arch emblazoned *Tara* at the entrance to their driveway on the outskirts of Pine Bough subdivision. The house broods at the top of the hill, exactly the way it looked in the David O. Selznick film: complete with upright, shining columns. Tara is on the list of sightseeing attractions the Chamber of Commerce publishes, a list which includes the Civil War cannon sitting on the courthouse lawn, the University football stadium, and the portrait of the governor displayed in the lobby of the Holiday Inn. Tourists sometimes make their way up the twisting half-mile drive and sit, staring at Tara from inside their air-conditioned cars. There isn't much to see. The heavy drapes along the high french windows are always drawn. The family doesn't even use the front door, they come and go through the kitchen, which, unlike the kitchen from the movie, is resplendent with two microwaves and Spanish tile. An island in the middle, a dutch oven, a griddle, a Cuisinart, a state-of-the-art gas stove. Jimbo's mother used to like to cook.

Jimbo walks through his parents' house. His mother's arthritic maid is polishing silver at the broad expanse of the dining room table. Jimbo stands uncomfortably at the door.

"How are you, Lima?" he says, conscious, as he has been for years, of how silly he feels calling her Lima, when her real name is Evangalina and she is seventy-three years old; gray-haired and stooped, with fallen arches. Lima, saddled everywhere, all over town, with the nickname the child of one of her employers gave her, who knows when, back in the sixties. When he was little, he and his sister called her Lima Bean.

"Tolerable," she tells him, squinting at his reflection in the immense silver-plated tray she's holding in her hands. "Your mama's in the bed."

Jimbo shifts his feet.

"Um," he says noncommittally. "I reckon I won't bother her then. Just swung by to see how y'all were getting along . . ." He stops and listens to the silence of the house, the hum of appliances in the kitchen, the underlying presence of central air-conditioning.

"She's not feeling bad, is she?" he continues.

"No," Lima says. Her voice trails off. "Just tired." He and Lima both know why his mother is in bed at three o'clock on a sunny Wednesday afternoon. His eyes search out the decanter gleaming on the sideboard.

"I see you on the TV," Lima reports to him abruptly. "You look real good up there in your suit. Everybody's awful proud, you know?"

"Well, thank you, Lima," he says. "Tell mama I came by, okay?" He turns toward the door.

"Could you do something for me, Jimbo?"

He turns back around.

"Could you carry that vacuum upstairs? My back is acting up real bad."

"Sure," he says agreeably.

As he turns the car around on the circular drive, his police radio crackles. When he goes down the hill, the yellow legal pads on the passenger seat slide onto the floorboards. At the foot of it, he turns on Pine Bough Drive absently, thinking about Lima, thinking about the four other days a week she spends, at other people's houses. Does she say what's going on at Tara? He feels certain that she does, knows it from the way his mother's friends hurl their shopping carts in front of his out at the Winn-Dixie.

"And how's your mama, Beauregard?" Their voices swoop and chatter. "I haven't seen her for a while. Now y'all just tell me if you need any help with anything, you hear?" And then they inform him that they've seen him do the weather, or cover the student protest outside the University main building, in the drizzling rain.

"We're all so proud of you, Beauregard," they say. Why? he wonders. Because in high school he had broken into their houses while they were at Lake Lanier and stolen all their silver? Because his father had said he was taking him hunting and had lured him in the car and up to Alto, juvenile detention? Having tried Tough Love, Charter River, and the broad side of his meaty hand? Because Jimbo had done all that and ended up the Channel Seven weather man?

And then they say, "Your sister . . ." and he turns his cart abruptly. Leaves them with the words still caught back in their throats, their hands full of summer squash or Stove Top stuffing. He's heard what they have to say before. They stop him when he's waiting in line at the bank. They stop him when he's pumping gas into his car. Their voices are full of conspiratorial concern. They think that Nadine should go home, think that Jimbo, somehow, should *make* her.

"Your sister . . ." they say. They pause delicately. "Well, I don't know how to put it. She wears the strangest *clothes*. And have you seen her *hair* lately?" They've seen her walking down the street, seen the leather jacket shrugged on over the black slip. The torn-up fishnet stockings and the red lipstick. It bothers them. They think she should go home. They think they know what's going on. But they *don't*—Jimbo won't make her. He remembers the night, when he was still in high school, when he walked downstairs into the kitchen, and Nadine was standing, backed up against the kitchen door. She was only eight or nine.

"Not good enough," their mother told her. "You're just not good enough." Her voice was calm. "You'll *never* be good enough," their mother promised. Jimbo's brand-new pickup truck was gleaming in the rain outside the kitchen door. He took his little sister by the arm.

"Where are we going?" she asked him.

"Oh, I don't know." They sat inside the steamy cab of the pickup, pulled up at a convenience store. He drank a six-pack while she sniffled in the corner, yawning. Then he took her home.

He tried to get her to live with him, took the job at Channel Seven, here in town, right after graduation, partially for that. He tries to give her money but usually she won't take it.

"Look, watch the drugs, okay?" he tells her. "Stay in school. Really. It'll end up being worth it."

She looks at him. Her face is blank. "You sound like a commercial." She is so far away, he can feel her drifting. It's like all she wants to do is erase the fact that she had ever had a family.

"You didn't do it. Stay in school," she tells him. "You just got your G.E.D."

"Yeah, well, I regret that," he says shortly. He wants to shake her. He moves toward her and she flinches away from him, sitting with her arms wrapped around her knees on the worn-out sofa on the porch of the house she lives in.

He stops when he sees her jerk like that.

"Look. Just call me, anytime you need to. No matter what."

"Yeah, okay," she says. "I *like* living here."

James Beauregard Durham is the son of Little Beau, the star University quarterback of the class of '61. The grandson of Big Beau, who took over his father-in-law's legal practice in a building where there were two sets of restrooms, one labeled *white*, the other, *colored*, up until the early eighties. James Beauregard Durham the Third, he likes his job. Not the weather, which is just a rung on a broadcasting career ladder. Jimbo likes the reporting he does, likes the sudden calls. His mother's friends think they know everything about this town. But Jimbo really does. Knows the east side, out beyond the railroad tracks. Knows the city government beat downtown. Knows secrets terrible and good. Has seen the floaters' bodies when they pull them from the muddy river. Has thrown up in the bushes while the cops were watching. Knows this town like anything, like the backs of his hands (which are not meaty like his father's).

Will

Will Daniels keeps the lyrics of the song he wrote for the band that's getting airplay Scotch-taped to the dirty wall above his bed. Sometimes the girls he brings home notice it, sometimes they don't. But mostly they do. "What's that?" they ask him, usually in the morning, when the bedsheets smell like liquor and they're looking for their clothes, tangled in the blankets or lying on the floor. "Oh, that's the song I wrote with so-and-so," he says casually. They peer at it carefully and usually "Oh" is all they say, because everybody in town knows about so-and-so now, knows he's been on Letterman and Saturday Night Live. Will figures that the girls go home and scrabble through their records, looking for so-and-so's first album. If they do, they'll find out he's not lying, there's his name right there on the inner sleeve: Lyrics by Will Daniels.

"But you know how those guys are," he mentions, "I didn't get a cent." He runs his fingers down the spine of whatever girl it is who lies beside him on the bed. She either looks at him, relieved, or looks away.

"The song I did for the Barnburners, it did better," he explains. "Their album went platinum, you know?" He never tells them that his song is the one that's never played on the radio.

HAVE YOU HAD THE FULL DANIELS DEAL?—It's scrawled in a stall in the women's room down at the Club, like it's the FULL MEAL DEAL down at the Dairy Queen, which only costs two twenty-nine. But Will doesn't know that. He meets girls at a party or down at the Club and then he brings them home. He lights the stubby candles set on the floor around his bed. He puts Patti Smith on the tape player. And then the girls get up in the morning and sometimes they want to go to breakfast.

"I've got a lot of work to do," he explains. They look at him.

"I'll call you tonight," he reassures them, but then he almost never does. After the first time, it's never quite the same. He lets them out the front door and they go off down the sidewalk, looking sloppy and hungover. He goes back in the house and lies down on the bed. The fat palmetto bugs stalk around the grubby molding of the walls. He gets up and makes a cup of instant coffee or puts a piece of bread into the oven. Then the phone rings or it's time for his shift down at Dupree's. He walks down the Avenue, turns left at the corner, and heads toward downtown, squinting at the sun.

And then he's at Dupree's and it smells like mops and oysters. The busboy crouches on a milk crate, cleaning a pile of shrimp that never seems to end. He doesn't say anything to Will when he comes in the kitchen and hangs his coat up. He doesn't like Will much; he knows a girl who has cried about him more than once, cried when the busboy walked her home from somewhere, a winter's worth of parties. The busboy's face is pitted and his hair is lank on his forehead, but he really *liked* that girl, and every time he walked her home she'd shiver in the cold and lean up against him, but she was staring at the stars, the street, and thinking of Will Daniels.

Will goes behind the bar and fills up his coffee cup with vodka. If the manager comes in, he'll switch to coffee. He doesn't even grimace at the first sip, just takes the earring from his ear and puts it in his pocket. He preps some tables, folds some napkins, flirts with the waitresses when they come in, folding their coats and changing shoes. He's slept with two or three, and for a few days there's always *that* to get through, when they come in and their faces are deliberately scrubbed blank. When they turn toward him, he never knows exactly what it is they *want*, but then things will get busy: orders are backed up, plates broken, and then it seems like, finally, even *they've* forgotten.

Davey is prepping vegetables, his hair bundled up into a hairnet. His clothes always smell like fish. He keeps the radio above the triple sinks turned up until the restaurant opens. He stirs a pot of gumbo tenderly, runs his hands along the tins of spices. He's dreamy when he cooks. He's in some other place, not in this simmering kitchen, a place where the girls he'll meet at parties after work are soft and willing. The little paper tabs of acid nestled in his pockets burn like an extra heart, there and waiting.

When Will clocks in, there's somebody new washing dishes. He figures at first that it's just another high school boy, they come and go so fast, but then she turns from the sinks and grabs another bus-tray of dishes. She's a skinny, tired-looking girl with knobby elbows, and her T-shirt is spattered with water; he can see her nipples through it. Her hair is cut short and flattened with sweat and steam and grease.

After closing, she strains when she lifts the mop bucket full of steaming Pine-Sol'ed water. She leans all her weight into the mop, flings it out and pulls it back toward her. Everyone else has counted out their money and gone home, except for Davey, sitting on a stool and reading a day-old paper. Will hands her two damp dollars from his roll of tips and she shoves them in her pocket and keeps on mopping steadily. She says "Thanks," and her voice is raspy. He stands there a minute, watching the curve of her cheek, the ropy muscles in her arms: she's odd-looking, he thinks, but pretty.

"You need a ride someplace, when you get done?" he says suddenly, when she turns her head toward the floor, toward the bucket full of swirling, grayish water.

Davey scrapes his stool along the floor. "She doesn't need a ride," he says and says it harshly. "I'm taking her home." Will turns and looks. Davey's eyes are steady, measured, as if he knows Will, knows him better than their two years' worth of shifts together at Dupree's warrants. As if he's really saying, *this* girl is not for the likes of you. It irritates Will, the way Davey always does, the way he thinks he's king of this stupid, smelly kitchen, the way the waitresses say they like him, the way they sit down on stools when things are slow and tell him all their love-life problems.

"Well," he says. The girl looks up.

"I can take care of myself," she says sharply and throws herself into her mopping. "But Davey lives right by me." Will shrugs and puts his coat on.

"There's a party, out past the river," he says to Davey as he walks out, to put their relationship back where it belongs. Davey grunts and picks up his newspaper but he isn't really looking at it, he's looking at the girl, guardedly, as if he were her brother. And later, when Will leaves the party and is driving aimlessly, he sees them on the Avenue, close to his house. Davey pushes his bicycle and the girl's shoulders are hunched inside her torn-up leather jacket. She's just a kid, Will thinks, but maybe not. It's three a.m. and what is there on the Avenue but splintered, wooden rental houses? Not places where families live, mothers, fathers, normal people. Will's never seen anyone push a stroller down the Avenue. The weedy front yards along the street are never strewn with toys or swing sets.

Nadine

When Nadine left the first time, she didn't make it very far. "Dumb," she reminds herself now, thinking about it. "Nadine, you used to be so *dumb*." It was on a Saturday and it was easy enough to go; she just walked out the front door. She went down

through the subdivision toward the park along the lake. She
didn't know any other place to go. She sat on a bench until it got
dark, throwing rocks at the ducks sleeping on the dirty water. It
started getting cold. She walked back home. She thought maybe
they'd be eating dinner, wondering where she was. But dinner
wasn't started and no one had even noticed she'd been gone seven
hours.

The second time was different. Her mother sat at the dining
room table drinking bottles of white wine. The empty green jugs
were lined up in a row in the utility room.

"I'm going to the liquor store," her mother said. It was what
she had said every night, since the beginning of the summer. She
walked there with their dog trotting behind her. Now, when the
dog dug out of her pen, it was the liquor store she ran to—sitting
there beside the door until the cashier called and told them where
she was.

Nadine was still so dumb: she must have been fourteen. She'd
seen too many After School Specials. She and her mother stood
on the front steps.

"Don't you think maybe you're drinking more than maybe you
should?" she asked her mother. That was what they said on television. She tried to make her voice all soft and understanding. She
didn't know what it was she thought would happen. Maybe her
mother would look at her and then start crying. Put her arms
around her.

"What gives you the right to talk like that to me?" her mother
said. Her hand snaked out and swiped Nadine across the skull.
Nadine fell down, mostly from surprise. Her face was level with
her mother's feet, tucked neatly into white sandals. Each toenail
was pink and perfect, like a shell. Her mother reached down and
twined her hands in Nadine's hair and yanked. She slapped Nadine across the mouth and turned and walked into the house. Nadine heard the deadbolt click, the chain on the door rattle. She sat
down on the stairs and sniffled. The window to her bedroom flew

up. Her mother unlatched the screen. She dumped a dresser drawer out the window.

"Just get out," she shrieked. She flung Nadine's coat out. Nadine watched it land in the holly bush underneath the window. A hand reached out and latched the screen. Nadine stood there in the darkness.

She got her coat out of the bushes and walked down the driveway. She thought about the beginning of the summer, when she had come home from the swimming pool and her father was gone. Just not there anymore. Her mother hadn't said a word. Two weeks later, he had come and picked her up, asking her to meet him at the entrance to the subdivision. "To explain," he said.

Nadine got in the car and stared out of the window.

"You look like the Vietcong," he said. "A spy." It was supposed to be a joke, because she was dressed in black. Nadine didn't laugh. Her father started driving, drove through town and past the city limits sign.

"Where are you taking me?" Nadine said. "Where are you going?"

"I want you to know," her father told her, "that I will never let Brook come between us." Nadine didn't know who Brook was, a man or a woman. She could tell her father wanted her to ask him. She looked out the window. A gray horse was running in the field alongside the highway. Nadine watched that. They passed a beaten, silvered shack, porch sagging, pointed toward the road. I could live *there*, Nadine thought. I'd have that gray horse and a cat. I'd go down to that cow pond for water. I'd buy *Stalking the Wild Asparagus*. I'd eat the blackberries in the ditch in summer.

"Your mother is unstable," her father said. He cleared his throat. Nadine put her hands over her ears. She thought *gray horse   little shack   I'll get wood for my fireplace down beside the river   I'll find a shiny English saddle we'll ride along the fence the grass will be bent where the wind is blowing,* but she couldn't keep a hold on it. She thought about the time she was lying in bed and heard a thump, her mother screaming. *I hope you have a heart attack,* a voice suggested dully, *while you're in the middle of it.*

The first night she slept inside a laundromat. She asked a lady going into the beauty shop for two dollars for a pack of cigarettes and a cup of coffee. She walked all the way through town, toward the edges of the river. A man in a Buick stopped and asked her where she was going. She told him the high school, just to have a place to say. She got into his car.

"You don't really want to go there," he informed her. He fumbled in between his legs. The car pulled up at a stop light.

Nadine looked at his lap. "I'll cut it off," she warned him flatly. She leapt out of the car. The man looked startled.

"I didn't mean anything," he explained, but she was gone, running between the lanes of traffic.

Will

Within a week, the girl appears to know the ropes at Dupree's. She stands outside the kitchen door when it's slow inside, carefully pinching the coal off her half-smoked cigarette and laying it on the little window ledge to come back to later. She's taken over Davey's tinny radio and replaced his Grateful Dead with homemade tapes she brings in, pulling them out of the pockets of her leather jacket. The Sex Pistols, the Dead Kennedys. Davey doesn't seem to mind although he's always snarled any time Will has suggested changing stations.

When the first rush dies down, he goes in the kitchen to sort through the plates from the bussed tables, picking through the hushpuppies for pieces of fried fish to take home. She's sitting on a stool at the prep counter, eating a bowl of something, gumbo or shrimp creole. "What's that," she says, watching him drop pieces of fish into a grocery stack. "You eat that?" She grimaces.

"It's for my cat," he explains.

"You have a cat?"

He nods.

"What's it's name?"

"Tom," he tells her, shortly. She looks disappointed.

"Tom," she echoes. "What a name." He knows she means, what a *boring* name. He drops a piece of greasy fish into his paper bag.

"I saw this thing," he says abruptly, "on TV? It said if you give old people a cat, they live longer. If you give crazy people pets, it makes them happier."

"Really?" she says. "I'd like to have a cat. I'd name it Oregon or Baltimore, maybe Manhattan."

"Names of cities?"

"They're places that I've never been. I think they sound cool." Will shrugs.

"Once I had a cat named Jim Beam but my mother ran over him," she continues.

"On purpose?"

"I don't think so," She paused. "She was drunk." Her voice is casual. Will looks at her. She's scraping at the bottom of her bowl of gumbo with a spoon. Not looking like she's said anything important. But for a minute Will feels almost like she did, like they've traded something, some insider information.

"Will Daniels!" Davey yells. "Your fucking plates for table four have been under the hot-lamp for ten fucking minutes."

When Will comes back into the kitchen, she's standing by the sink. Davey is beside her, holding one of her arms stretched out above her head. Her hand is stuck into a plastic Baggie full of ice. Water, tinted pink, is running down her arm.

"What happened?"

Little drops of blood spatter the floor. Her white T-shirt is smeared with it.

"I stuck my hand into the sink," she says. "I couldn't see what was down in there." A knife is on the stainless steel counter.

"Somebody put a knife in it," Davey says, disgusted.

"Does it need stitches?"

"Probably," Davey says morosely.

"Well, take her to the hospital," Will says. It's what they've always done before. "They've got the insurance to cover it."

"No." The girl looks frightened.

"Can't," Davey explains. "She's not really on the payroll."

"It's illegal for me to be here, where they're serving liquor," the girl says softly. "I'm just fifteen. The owner hired me for a favor. I can't afford for him to have to fire me."

Davey lowers her hand and peers into the plastic Baggie.

"It's stopping bleeding, some," he says.

"Well, wrap it up," Will says. He wants somebody to do something. The Baggie full of bloody water is a bummer. The girl's face is very white.

"Can't," Davey says. "The first aid box was empty. I already checked."

"Well, *here,*" Will says in exasperation. "Go cook some fucking fish." He finds a clean towel. "I'll do it."

Davey looks at him. "Always ready, aren't you, Daniels?" he mutters, and Will knows suddenly that Davey *hates* him, maybe always has and that he's jealous, that he wants this skinny girl for something, even though he's all of thirty-five.

"There's orders up," he points out. Davey turns to the fryer reluctantly.

Will wraps the girl's hand in a towel. The cut looks like a fleshy mouth, curved in a crescent across her hand. He fumbles with the towel, trying to knot it.

"I can't wash dishes," she says suddenly, like she just realized it.

"It's okay," Will says. "It's pretty late. Not too much left to do. I'll mop the floor."

"But not just *tonight*," she says. Her voice is loud. He looks at her face. It's red and sweaty. "I can't do it tomorrow or the next. I gotta keep this job."

"The boss isn't so bad," he tells her. "He won't fire you just because you cut your hand. All the dishwashers cut themselves, okay?"

"Okay," she says, embarrassed. He puts an order on a tray. She's bent over the sinks, trying to load the washer with one hand.

When Will gets ready to clock out, she's sitting on a stool at the prep counter. "What's your name?" he asks her.

"Nadine."

"Well, Nadine," he asks her, "would you like a ride somewhere?"

"Okay," she says. She looks around the kitchen. Davey is in the storeroom. She slides off the stool and gets her leather jacket.

"You want some beer?" he says when they're driving down the Avenue.

"Okay."

"You want to go to my house?"

She shrugs.

Nadine

Will's house is cold and their feet are loud on the floorboards as they walk through to the kitchen. Paint peels from the grimy walls. The ceilings of the rooms they walk through are high and dark—the overhead wiring has never worked, in all the years that Will has lived there. She wonders why there isn't any furniture. There's a messy heap of blankets in the corner of the middle room, a cheap radio set on the windowsill. No pictures on the walls. He leads her to the kitchen for a cup of coffee that she doesn't really want. The milk he pours into her cup is clotted, thick and rotten. The plastic milk jug is the only thing she can see, behind his body, in the dirty refrigerator.

"I like to live alone," he tells her. His voice is loud in the empty room. Nadine doesn't know if she believes him because this isn't living alone, it's something else, like this falling-down old house is a Motel Six. He tells her that his ex-girlfriend got all the furniture when he moved out.

"Oh?" she says. "What was she like?"

"She was very smart. A graduate student in art history."

"Oh," Nadine says. "I'm an undergraduate in film," but then she remembers that he knows she's just fifteen.

"I say that sometimes," she says. "I've got to have a cover story."

"Well, do you like it? Film?"

"I guess," she says. "I like to go to movies." Will takes away their coffee cups and replaces them with two cans of beer. Nadine sits and watches him. She thinks how good-looking he is. His arms look very strong. He catches her staring at them. She looks away and walks into the bedroom.

"There's nothing on the walls," she comments, but then she sees the piece of paper tacked up over the bed and goes toward it.

"What's this?"

"Oh, just the song I wrote for so-and-so," he says casually. She turns toward him.

"Really?" Her eyes widen.

"Well, yeah."

But then he changes the subject.

"Do you want to take a shower? I've got to get the smell of Dupree's off me."

"Okay," she says. He walks toward the bathroom. She sits down on the bed to wait. He comes back into the bedroom.

"Are you coming?"

"Oh," she says. "You meant *together*." She looks startled.

"Well, not if you don't want to." He is suddenly embarrassed.

"I knew what you meant." She bends down and starts untying her shoes. "I just was checking." In the bathroom, she turns her back toward him when she pulls off her shirt. The towel is still wrapped around her hand. She stands inside the bathtub shivering and holds her arm out stiff, outside the shower curtain. The water pressure isn't very good. Will turns out the light and lights a candle.

"That's better, right?"

"Yeah," she says. She tries to smile. He bends his head toward her. She closes her eyes. He keeps his open. The water runs over her face. The towel drops. She lays her hands against his back.

"Are you on anything?" he asks her finally.

"On anything? Like drugs?"

"Like birth control."

"Oh. No," she says. "I'm sorry."

"Are you a virgin?"

"God," she says. "Of course not."

"Well, that's okay then," he says, relieved. "I've got something."

She can't ever go to sleep. The ceiling is so high it feels like there's too much empty space between it and the mattress on the floor. She listens to him breathe. He grinds his teeth and says things. She puts her arm across his body. He rolls away from her until he shakes it off. She thinks about his house. If she lived here, she'd go around to yard sales until they had some furniture. She'd hang up curtains. She could bake bread and cook big pots of things in the yellow kitchen. She'd get him new shirts. The ones he wears to Dupree's are always ragged. He has that car, though. They could go places, camping. New York, California. The pecans rain down on the tin roof. They sound to her like bullets.

After a while, light filters through the blanket nailed to the tall windows. She watches him. His head is hidden underneath his pillow. The sheet is wrapped around his feet. His body is beautiful, unmarked. She wishes he would wake up.

Outside the window, there's the sound of cracking wood and voices shouting. She pulls back the blanket tacked over the window. The house next door is splintered wreckage. She hadn't really noticed it the night before. Three men stand in a semicircle in the driveway, smoking cigarettes and drinking coffee. A pickup truck is backed up to the steps. Its bed is stacked with doors and window sashes. Two men come out the front door and ease a dark wooden mantelpiece onto the top of the pile. A yellow bulldozer is grinding through the muddy yard. One of the men throws down his cigarette and picks up a brick. He weighs it in his hand, still talking, then tosses it toward a window. The men beside him laugh. The glass shivers, shatters. Through the empty window frame, Nadine can see the faded, ripped wallpaper inside, the lighter patch above the mantel where a picture must have hung. Will moves and opens up his eyes. He looks amazed to see her there.

"Did you sleep?" he says.

"Not really. They're tearing down the house next door, you know?"

He shrugs. "They've taken all that's good. It's just a heap of rotten lumber."

She looks back out the window. "It looks like it was pretty. Once, I mean."

Will folds the pillow underneath his head. "Yeah, maybe."

She watches him. "Hey," she says tentatively, "do you want to go to breakfast?"

"I can't," he says flatly. He doesn't look at her. "I've got a lot to do." He pauses. "I tell you what, though," he says finally. "Leave me your phone number, okay? I'll call you tonight or something."

Davey

Someone is knocking on his door, pulling at the screen, trying to get it open. He looks at the clock beside the bed. It's eight o'clock. He pulls back the tie-dyed sheet hung over the window and spots Nadine standing at the door, huddled in her leather jacket. He goes to it to let her in.

"What is it?"

She wavers back and forth on her feet. "Hey," she says brightly. "Let's smoke some pot. Okay?" She forces a smile.

He runs his hands through his hair and yawns. "At eight a.m.?" He looks at her. "Well, okay," he says finally.

They sit down on the bed. He pulls his bong and tray from underneath it. She reaches over and picks out a weedy stem and puts it in her mouth, watching him intently while he tamps the weed into the bowl. He gives it to her first. She inhales and holds her breath. He does the same, then expels the smoke, a filmy stream that mixes with his words.

"You go home with him? Last night?"

She gets up and walks around the room. Picks things up off the mantel and lets them drop.

"Who?" she says and lights a cigarette.

"Will Daniels," he says flatly.

"Oh, no way. That asshole." She throws her cigarette onto the floor and steps on it.

"Don't do that," he tells her mildly.

She whirls around. "I'll do what I want." she tells him. "Do you have any beer?"

And then she lies there on the bed. She can hear the trains down in the gullies. Davey's body is over hers, his hands are on her breasts. Think about the trains, she tells herself. Think of where they're going. A dog is howling somewhere.

"Are you all right?" he asks her.

"I'm fine," she says.

She dreams about the railroad tracks that slice through the muddy brush and vagrant camps along the river, twin filaments of silver that can never pull her anywhere. When Davey wakes up, he turns on the television set beside his bed. A body's been found face down, floating in the muddy river. Her brother looks toward the camera. His face is grim. He's reporting.

Jimbo

He's meeting Nadine for lunch. He let her choose where, a greasy place downtown. She's there when he comes in, sitting at a corner booth beside the window, turned toward a long-haired man in an army fatigue jacket who drops her hand and slouches away from the table when Jimbo comes toward them.

"Who's that?" he asks her. She looks sad and tired.

"Nobody." She's looking at the menu.

"You okay?"

"Yeah, I'm fine." The waitress comes to take their order.

"I saw you on the news this morning," she says after a while.

"Yeah?"

"What's it like?" she asks him. "Seeing dead people? What do they look like?"

He stirs his coffee. "They look dead, I guess," he tells her carefully. "The first time, I threw up. You know? But now I don't feel much. I mean, I feel *sad*. I mean it's *awful*. But not the way I did at first." He thinks of the churned-up mud he and the cameraman and cops had slid through, marching past the charred wood in a fire-ring and a row of mismatched coffee cups lined up on the flat rocks as if the person who had left them there thought he was doing something with a purpose, as if he thought that he was setting up a home.

Nadine

The waitress puts down their orders. Nadine shoves her plate to the middle of the table. All the times she's come to May's, she's never noticed the placemats before. Hers has a photograph of a beaming woman wearing a bright, orange-colored dress on it. A plate of fake-looking eggs is extended in her hands toward a fat little boy sitting at a table. It's like something off of *Leave It to Beaver*. In cheery yellow letters underneath the picture are the words EGGS FOR YOUNG AMERICA. She traces the letters with her finger.

Jimbo's quiet, watching her.

"That guy who was sitting here," he says, "you seeing him?"

She shrugs. "I don't know. Maybe." She raises her head and lights a cigarette, then turns to look at her reflection in the window, pushing at her hair with her fingers.

"Who is he?" Jimbo asks her.

"A guy," she tells him. "A guy I know."

Her brother clears his throat.

"Listen, Nadine," he says. His face earnest and awkward. "Don't," he says, "make people like that your family."

"It doesn't matter," she says. She squints and blows smoke at her reflection in the window. She can see a reflection of everything in the restaurant. Jimbo has started eating his hamburger. The waitress is coming toward them with more coffee. She pulls a drag of smoke into her lungs. It hurts, but that's okay.

"It's no big fucking deal," she says, smashing her cigarette out in the ashtray and pulling her plate toward her. "It's no big fucking deal," she says again. Her shoulders squared, her chin determined, she bends her head toward her plate—she knows for sure that she believes it.

The Gulf

One

*U*sually, there's a line of girls at the foot of the club's stage, close-packed, lunging forward, nights when the band headlines. When Leroy jerks back, the line of girls jerks forward, a chain, he always says, a half-smile on his lips—does he mean it, is he joking?—he likes to yank. But tonight the dance floor's almost empty and the sparse crowd sitting at the tables is paying more attention to the television screen behind the bar than to the way he's singing "Needles and Pins."

Jolene sits at the bar, dangling her feet. She chews a straw, she crunches ice, she shreds a paper napkin. Up on the stage, Leroy snarls tiredly and paces. He stalks across the stage and back, the mike cord black behind him like a snake. Under the harsh lights, sweat soaks his thin black T-shirt clean through. The ceiling fans above him barely stir the smoky air.

It seems to Jolene that he's edgy, tenser than he would be if the club were crowded. He swings his guitar up above his canted hip and stares out, surly, at the empty chairs. Even though she's seen the band a hundred times, the way Leroy starts a show still pulls her in; those first few harsh chords and the way he swings the mike stand out toward the audience and back, a precarious half-circle.

But the funny thing is, he says he can't see anything from up there, that it's all a blur beyond the wall of heat slanting from the stage light fixtures to the floor. Although he glances, quick, toward the bar as if he knows exactly where Jolene is sitting. Although he stares out at the crowd as if he's singling someone out. And always, every show, there's some girl out there on the floor, pressed up against the stage and amps, her head up-tilted toward him, thinking he's looking right at her, whether he really is or not. When he looks out at the dance floor, the girl starts moving wildly, her eyes following every gesture, every slashing chord he makes.

But he says he can't see any of it, and Jolene knows how badly he needs glasses. The way he moves up on the stage, it's just an exercise, like chords he practices over and over at their apartment in the bathroom because that's where the sound is better. His gestures are just another thing that works, something else somebody taught him. He turns his back on the audience, he pivots on his heels. It's like he's behind a pane of glass.

"I can see," her friend Carla had said, the first time Jolene dragged her into the club to see the band, "some sort of wildness in him." *But that wasn't what I wanted to show you*, Jolene wanted to say suddenly. *That's not him at all—you've been suckered too.* After the show was over, he came up to their table shyly. Jolene was struck by two very different things about him: he had a certain gentleness, but over it there always was the hard patina he had worked, for so long, to keep on.

Two

Leroy had figured no one would show up for the gig. "If it was up to me," he told Jolene when she walked into their apartment after work, "we'd cancel." The television set was on; fuzzy figures wavered on the screen. The bed was strewn with newspapers. The figures on the screen appeared to be on the steps of the state capitol. "If it was up to me . . ." he said again. He cocked his head. "We'd be down at the capitol instead." A solemn newscaster appeared.

"It's funny," Jolene said slowly, looking at the screen. "What's going on, it's not a war, is it?"

Leroy looked at her and shrugged. He walked toward the television set and hit it with the flat of his hand, to clear up the reception.

They watched as soldiers in the desert appeared on the screen. "You poor dumb fuckers," Leroy said, addressing their wavering images. "I wonder if you had any idea what you were getting into?"

The screen changed, flashed to Baghdad, with greenish bursts of light above the buildings.

"Shit . . ." Leroy said. He and Jolene stood there for a minute, quiet, their bodies angled toward the screen. It was, Jolene realized suddenly, as if they were trying to decipher something faint and far away, something in another language. Words that were familiar, recognizable, but something their ears were not completely attuned to, yet.

Three

"I don't even know where any of these places *are*," Jolene comments to Carla, when they stand outside the club, smoking cigarettes. Every time someone opens the door behind Carla's back, the sound of Leroy's voice comes sliding out. "I don't know which of these countries we're supposed to like."

"Neither do I," Carla says. She'd never dream of telling Jolene she doesn't really care. Jolene is always much too serious. "Let's go back in before they quit playing," she says suddenly. "I want to dance to one last song."

There always is a moment for Jolene, a moment when she steps into the club, into the acrid, smoky air, when she looks over at the stage and Leroy seems to be a stranger. He doesn't even look like someone she would want to meet. But then the moment passes, Leroy stares toward her like he sees her, and there's a bravado about his boots that makes her think his face seems sad and worried. Behind him, Jalapeño and Benjy both have picked tonight to go all out—they're wearing matching tacky bolo ties and the dark red sharkskin suits they lucked into at the Daughters of the Texas Revolution yard sale, the weekend all of them drove out to Llano. Jalapeño's suit doesn't fit at all. He picks at his bass, a cigarette between his lips, his chin jutting. Sweat drips from his forehead. Benjy's suit, on the other hand, fits him perfectly, since he's short and sort of round. While Jolene watches, he pulls out his mirror shades and sets them on his nose with a flourish.

When Jalapeño bends down to adjust his amp, he almost wavers on his feet. Leroy is watching him closely out of the corner of his eye. Jolene wonders if she should ask the bartender for a glass of water for Jalapeño—or would the pause when she holds it out and Benjy and Leroy turn toward him, eyes measuring whether he can keep his feet, embarrass him? Leroy shouts hoarsely into the mike. The sweat runs down his face. The Telecaster against his hip is dark and polished, flashing dangerously under the hot stage lights, the color of gun barrels. Leroy likes an understated look, he has explained to Jolene. She looks down at his feet. His boots are black; the pointed toes look like weapons, and the heels make every movement sexual when he moves across the stage. When he has a case of pre-gig nerves, he polishes his boots for hours; to a high, hard gloss, the way they did it in the army. It's the only thing, he swears, about that time that sticks.

Four

"There he is," Carla says suddenly. She cranes her neck.

"Who?" Jolene says, her attention still on the stage.

"Little Dex."

"God," Jolene says. She looks at Carla. "I thought that was over. You still *like* him?"

"I don't know," Carla says vaguely. "Sort of. I mean, yes. He looks so *tough*."

"Too much speed," Jolene observes. "And he needs a haircut."

"He holds himself like he don't need nobody, you know?" Carla says. "He looks like he's just fine all on his own."

"He's gross," Jolene says. "No offense, Carla."

Carla shrugs. Her fingers pull the label from her beer bottle. She rolls the paper into little balls.

"Well, who's nice, then?" she says sullenly.

Jolene looks around. "Jalapeño's nice," she says after a minute.

Carla stares up at the stage. "He's okay," she says. "But sometimes he seems spacy."

"So?" Jolene says impatiently. "Little Dex is an asshole. What would you rather have?"

"God, Jolene," Carla says, "what kind of question is that?"

"Jalapeño's a nice guy," Jolene tells her. "Just talk to him some time. It's not like you have to marry him."

It suddenly occurs to Carla that maybe Jolene thinks Jalapeño's cute herself. She looks slantwise at her but Jolene's head is tilted toward the stage, her eyes following the movements of Leroy's feet. "Maybe," Carla says. "We'll see." She stares at the stripped-off spot on her bottle. "Maybe I *like* unfriendly people," she says suddenly, under her breath. "Maybe I think nice is boring." She gives Jolene another sideways look, up through her hair. Jolene's got a cigarette dangling from one hand and she looks like she's just hanging out, like she's cool and doesn't care—but Carla knows for a fact she's memorized the words to every song the band plays.

Five

Right after Jalapeño had started playing with the band, Leroy left the van with him so he could fix the carburetor.

"I can't believe he screwed it up like that," Jolene said, after two weeks, when the van was still sitting in Jalapeño's front yard, stained with leaves and tree sap. "I can't believe you let him. I thought you said this guy knew all about cars."

"Look," Leroy said. "He does. He just works kind of slow."

"What's the problem?" Jolene asked curtly. "He doesn't even have a job."

"Things are bad for Jalapeño."

"Like how?" Jolene asked. She'd had to ride the bus to work for two weeks.

"Okay," Leroy said finally. He sighed. "This is a secret, now. Promise you won't tell Carla or let him know I told you."

Jalapeño, he explained to her, had done *his* time in the navy. It was weird, the way the two of them had both dropped out of school to enlist; the way when they got out, they'd both ended up in Austin. Jalapeño had been on a hulking piece of metal that floated in the Mediterranean. Signing up, Leroy said slowly, was a way to leave the shit at home behind.

This is what that day was like. Jalapeño can only really describe it when he's smoked a lot of pot. The way he and M.J. Darryl had just been down in the hangar bay, working on the ejector seat in the cockpit of a Tomcat. Outside, the water of the Mediterranean gleamed, reflecting like a mirror. The carrier purred under Jalapeño's feet, and when he heard M.J.'s stomach growl, he wondered how long it would be until lunch.

The only sound that could have warned him was a sudden,

sucking puff. It had never occurred to him to imagine what it would sound like if the ejectors in a seat misfired while he had his head bent over them. If it had, he would have expected the noise to be much louder. The seat traveled upward and barely clipped him on the chin, hurling him backward. He caught a second's glimpse of M.J.'s body propelled up toward the ceiling.

As fragile as an egg was what he'd always heard about the human skull. Not his, not after that: sometime during the weeks he couldn't quite remember, the doctors at the VA hospital had inserted a metal plate where the back of his skull had been. They had tidily wired his loosely hanging jaw. They kept the six snapped ribs from puncturing his laboring lungs. He was, they told him, very lucky. M.J.'s body had landed limply after it hit the curved steel ribs of the hangar.

When he was still in the hospital, Jalapeño wondered what had happened to the stack of *Screw* magazines M.J. had kept under his bunk. They weren't the kind of thing you'd want your mom to know. Weren't the memory you'd plan to leave her with. He wondered why it had been M.J. who died when he—somehow, miraculously—hadn't. But then, after awhile, he decided it wasn't such a good idea to wonder about M.J. anymore.

Once he got back home, the heat did something to his head. He went up to the VA hospital in Waco, where a doctor handed him a sheaf of prescriptions and listed all the things he shouldn't do. He shouldn't ride a motorcycle, or drink, or smoke, or drive a car. Heavy exertion, the doctor said, raising the volume of his droning voice with a meaningful look, could bring on a grand mal seizure. Jalapeño wondered about sex. *Could he . . .* he asked finally. The doctor stared past his shoulder. He would have to be, the doctor said, very, very careful.

After that, sometimes, the pressure in his skull built up until his head felt like the skin of a balloon blown to bursting. He wasn't sure if it was from the metal plate or from the things that he kept thinking. Smoking pot was the only thing that stopped it—that, or walking, sometimes. He sat on the front porch of the house and strummed at his guitar. Sometimes he'd work on a neighbor's car, or some girl's he liked, but it always seemed like when he finished there were too many screws and nuts he couldn't keep track of left over. The girls looked at him skittishly when they saw how many things he forgot to put back in their cars. Their eyes always traveled to the faint streak of scar scraped up under his hairline at the base of his skull.

So mostly he lived off his disability checks and walked all over town, hands shoved deep into the pockets of his flight jacket. He walked slowly, leaving the house early in the morning. He came home late in the afternoon. There didn't seem to him to be a single reason for any kind of hurry.

Six

When Leroy gets offstage, he's wired. He takes a swig from Jolene's beer and shifts his weight from one foot to the other.

"Hey, Carla, how you doing?" he says after a minute, nodding his head toward her. He looks at Jolene. "Be back in a minute," he tells her and moves back to the stage to start wrapping cords and pulling wires.

Jalapeño is standing on the edge of the stage, looking almost lost, looking like he had been about to do something that he's now forgotten. He catches Jolene's eye and climbs off the stage and walks toward them.

"Hey," he says and sits down. Jolene can smell his sweat. She puts her hand on his leg. The muscles in it tremble.

"Are you okay?" she asks him.

"Fine," he says. He gives Carla a nervous smile.

"Want some water?" Jolene asks him, pushing her plastic cup toward him.

Leroy walks back over to them. "The van's all packed," he announces. "You want a ride, Jalapeño?"

Jalapeño shakes his head. He stares at the television set above the bar, the lumbering jeeps, the swirling, sliding jets, the interviews with fighter pilots. Without the band to mask it, the newscast's brand-new, faintly oriental lead-in music is so loud it almost shakes the glasses on the shelf beside the screen.

"I'm going to walk," he says, bending over for his bass, "if y'all will take my amp and drop it off at my house tomorrow."

"Sure," Leroy says. He pauses, watching him. "Are you okay?"

Jalapeño nods. "Yeah," he says slowly. "It's just, I don't know, maybe it's this . . ." He jerks his head toward the television set.

"Yeah," Carla says suddenly. She lights a cigarette and looks at him. "It's kinda spooky."

Jolene looks at her. She knows Carla doesn't give a shit about what's on TV. Carla returns her stare blandly.

"See," Jalapeño says. He doesn't look at Leroy, he doesn't look at anybody really, just lowers his eyes and watches Carla's feet. "I watched TV all day. I just want to get away from the news for a little while." He raises his eyes and looks straight at Carla. "Want me to walk you home?" he asks her formally.

"Okay," Carla says and then she looks surprised—both at the question and her answer. She looks over at Jolene and raises her eyebrows, as if to say, *Well, okay, what now?* But at the same time she's thinking of Jolene's hand on Jalapeño's leg and the way both she and Leroy had asked him if he was okay.

She leans toward Jalapeño. "How'd you know where I live?" she asks him.

Jolene sets her glass down suddenly and stands up. It annoys her, the obvious way Carla is flirting. "Have fun, y'all," she tells them. She doesn't even want to watch it.

Seven

What is it like? Jolene thinks when she and Leroy are driving home, the sound of the radio filling up the van.

What is it like, the things they do; to stand inside a plane that's scoured out by wind? To cling to a guy wire making dirty jokes to cover up the fact that your face is sort of pale and you weren't able to eat breakfast? With Fort Benning, Georgia, spread out underneath you and the film they showed unwinding in your head and the lecture where they dropped the dummy from the top of the tower to illustrate that *this was how you died, it was all so easy.* What was it like to hurl yourself forward into the wind buffeting the plane, knowing that all the ground wanted was to rise to meet you?

Before Leroy, she had gone out with other guys who had been in the service. None of it was serious. Nick, with *Semper Fi* tattooed on one arm. Edward, recently discharged. Their stories all seemed sort of the same. Sometimes she forgot which one a certain person told her. They all went in and they were scared and most of the time they hated it. They did things she could not imagine forcing herself to do.

Eight

Leroy says he can't understand why skydiving is a sport. Why anyone would do it just for fun. He says it out of the blue—they're home in bed and she's about to fall asleep. *Were you afraid?* she asks him, *back then, when you had to parachute?* and the answer comes back slowly: *yes.* But it kept you so pumped up. Half of it was drudgery but half of it was such a rush. Everything seemed boring when he came back home, working 12 to 7 at a convenience store.

What was it like to be seventeen years old, in the middle of the desert in a foreign country?

"It was just like a job," he says. "I mean, I did it of my own free will and then they paid me."

Nine

Overseas, he frequented the greasy alleys where drugs changed hands.

Overseas, he tells her while they lie in bed, he delivered a Bedouin woman's baby without the aid of any sort of anesthesia.

"The stuff that went down over there," he says abruptly, getting up for a cigarette, "it changed things." He pauses. "I know how that sounds. Like I'm sappy." He sits on the edge of the bed, squinting, staring out into the darkened room.

"But I was only seventeen, you know?" he says, "Into 'Ballad of the Green Berets' and all that crap. I was the one who decided on the Special Forces. I thought it was going to do something to me, that it was going to make me hard, like John Wayne maybe. It was supposed to make me strong. Before I left for training, I was just a dishwasher in a restaurant. My stepfather kept telling me he couldn't wait until I was eighteen so he could make me leave the house. I wanted to do *something*. You know, just anything. It didn't matter what. The army's what the guidance counselors say if they look down at your folder and see you're taking things like shop. If they recognize your name because you hang out in the parking lot and cut too many classes. My mother cried when I left, but I think she was relieved." He shrugs. "I mean, she had a brand-new husband."

It was out on patrol that he delivered the Bedouin woman's baby, in an army tent. The sergeant fainted when the baby's head emerged.

"The crowning," Leroy says. "I think that's what you call it."

There hadn't been a medic to take over. After Leroy delivered the baby, he went outside and threw up for what seemed like hours, lying in the sticky sand outside.

"Why?" Jolene asks him softly. "Because you thought it was disgusting?"

"That wasn't it at all," he says. "All that screaming hurt. I never had imagined . . ."

Ten

In Jalapeño's bedroom, the bed is strewn with car parts and the direction sheets from boxes of model airplanes. He shoves an empty cardboard box onto the floor and backs through the door into the kitchen to make coffee. Carla sits awkwardly on the edge of the bed. The walls are grimy; there's a big black thumbprint on the door frame just above the corner of the bed. But the bed's made up and army-issue neat, as if Jalapeño actually bounces quarters on it.

"I like to fix things," he explains when he comes back just as she picks up one of the wrenches sitting on the bedside table next to a greasy distributor. She looks at him and sips her coffee.

"Is it okay?" he asks her after he sits down beside her on the bed.

"What?"

"The coffee. Is it okay?"

"Yeah. It's fine. I mean, it's coffee." He doesn't really smile.

"Did Jolene tell you?" he asks abruptly. "Did she say?"

"Tell me what?"

"What it is with me."

"She said you were nice," she tells him. What is it that he's going to tell her, starting it off this way, like a confession? There's always something that you have to know beforehand. Is it a disease? Or maybe that he's married. She shakes a cigarette out of her pack and waits.

"This is what it is," he says. He reaches awkwardly for her hand and places it against the back of his head. "Can you feel it?"

She frowns. Her fingers are against a puckered ridge of skin, the thin, raised seams of intersecting scars.

"I've got a metal plate," he says. "It happened in the navy." He looks at her steadily and reaches into his back pocket and pulls out his wallet.

"The doctors say I might go into a seizure if I indulge in any strenuous physical activity. It's not like they happen very much, okay? But if one ever did, all you'd have to do is stick my wallet in between my teeth, like this." He gestures with the wallet. "So I won't bite my stupid tongue off. You don't have to call 911 or anything. It's not like that. I mean, you could, though, if you were scared, if you wanted."

He places the wallet carefully on the quilt between them. Carla stares at it.

"I've got to tell you this," he says finally. "You think I like it? I never know whether to wait . . . I mean, wait for what? So I just tell people first off." He looks down at his hands and then stands up. "Look, I'll just take you home," he says hastily. He picks her purse up off the floor and hands it to her. "Where's your coat?"

"What're you doing?"

He looks down at the floor. "It's more than you can deal with, right?"

She's angry that his reading of her is pretty accurate. "Is that why you always tell people first off? Some sick sort of test? To see if they can take it?"

"Don't you get it? I couldn't even sleep with you. It's all the medicine or something. You always have so many boyfriends. Jolene's always saying *and Carla's seeing so-and-so,* and it's always someone different. And then, sometimes I see you, out somewhere with some guy . . . ." He stops. "I just wanted you to know it couldn't be like that."

"Like what? First you say something *might* happen if you do it, then you just say you can't."

"I was just trying to explain," he says after a minute.

"Explain what?"

"The last girl I really liked, she . . ." He stops.

She tries to think of a way to ask it. "Is it that you're scared of what might happen?"

"Not *scared*," he says quickly. "It's just, sometimes I have dreams, you know? I'm back there in the hangar-bay and there's this noise, like something breaking. I never heard that when it happened, in real life, but in this dream it's so loud. And I think, *Is that me? Or is it someone else?* And I'm so grateful—*I'm fine*—it's just something dropped, a wrench. Someone else's bad luck, somebody else's problem." He looks at her. "I mean," he says, "I'm *glad*."

Eleven

In high school, Carla had had a boyfriend who worked as a dishwasher at Red Lobster. The boyfriend, whose name was Jeremy, had long hair. This is just what she remembers from the vague picture of him she still keeps in her mind. She doesn't have a single photograph of him. He had been too stoned to remember to get his yearbook portrait taken. She can't remember if his eyes were blue or brown.

When Carla started going out with Jeremy, he gave her a sterling silver ring set with a polished tiger's-eye. It wasn't her style at all—she suspected he had bought it for a previous girlfriend she had seen walking down the hall, a hippie chick who had long straight hair and still wore bellbottoms.

When she broke up with him two months later, they had been sitting in her first car, a mustard-colored El Camino, in the Red

Lobster parking lot. He wrenched the ring off her finger, rolled down the window and hurled it to the pavement. He got out of the car and stalked up and down. When he spotted the ring, he ground it underneath the heel of his Dingo boot.

"Why do you want to break up?" he turned and shouted toward the window.

"I just don't like you anymore," she said. Her voice was cool. She felt enclosed, contained, inside the El Camino. His face was red; she caught a glimpse of his underwear when he bent over to pick up what was left of the crushed ring and fling it toward the Dempsey dumpster.

For a week or so she had had her eye on his best friend, Bruce, who was still inside Red Lobster, bussing his last tables. The night before, the three of them had driven out to Lexington's, a bar that never carded, and when Jeremy went up to the counter to get another pitcher of beer, Bruce had pressed his leg against hers, underneath the table.

When had she stopped liking Jeremy? She can't quite remember. Was it when the three of them bought three bottles of red wine and Jeremy hung his head, retching, out the window of the car, parked down beside the lake? When she stopped at his house to drop him off, she planned to leave him at the end of the driveway. "You ought to take him inside," Bruce had said. "He's so fucked up, he can't even get his shoes off."

"You take him in. You're his best friend," she had said.

"Yeah, but you're his girlfriend."

Or maybe it had been when they had all gone swimming and the jagged rocks along the creek were slick and Jeremy had fallen. Bruce snickered, and she hated the way Jeremy looked at her when he scrambled up and both his knees were scraped raw, bleeding. He wanted *something* from her. The way he looked at her tried to pull it from her.

Back then, things always seemed different before she slept with them. Every time she met someone, she thought maybe this time it would all work out okay—before she slept with them, it seemed like she loved them madly. Sometimes it lasted a little while after they started sleeping together, but then one day she would look at them and they would seem so dumb. They would be wearing tennis shoes without any socks, which looked retarded. They might have missed a patch of stubble when they shaved. But worst of all, they started looking at her like they counted on her for something. Like they felt bad or shy or awkward and wanted her to be some kind of cheerleader, convincing them they were okay.

Twelve

Jolene wakes up so wired she doesn't even need a cup of coffee.

"I wonder what happened between Carla and Jalapeño last night," she says when she feels Leroy move beside her.

"Is it any of your business?"

"I'd hate it if Carla hurt his feelings." There are two little worry lines between her eyebrows.

"There's nothing you can do about it."

"I know," she says slowly. "But I've been Carla's friend since high school. You know how she is. If she was going to be with Jalapeño, she'd have to really like him. He doesn't have, you know, any *style*. He's not hip or anything."

"What are you doing, worrying about them?"

"She's going to hurt his feelings. Sleep with him and blow him off."

"He's grown."

"Yeah," she says. "Maybe." She doesn't sound convinced. "They're both by themselves, you know?" she says after a minute. "They ought to be with someone."

"Why?" he says.

"Because," Jolene says. She flounders. "Because that's how it's supposed to be?"

Leroy wraps the quilt around her. He isn't even listening. "Let's go somewhere," he suggests. "Get out of town. We'll stop by Jalapeño's if you want. To see if Carla's there. Look," he tells her, "everything'll be okay."

Thirteen

Jalapeño's house droops to one side; the window frames slant into the walls. Sometimes it seems like all the people Jolene and Leroy know live in houses just like this, with weedy yards and rotten boards and faucets that don't work. It's gotten so Jolene hates the gassy smell of wood that's gotten wet too many times. She and Leroy walk gingerly up the stairs to the front porch.

Carla's sitting in a ratty chair pressed up against the wall, her legs stretched out in front of her, propped up on the splintered porch railing.

"Hey," Jolene says, and Carla's face, when she turns it toward her, is veiled somehow and blank and shuttered. Things aren't the way they used to be, back before Leroy came along, when they both were single. Then, Carla would show up at Jolene's apartment early in the morning and Jolene would start a pot of coffee. Carla would lie down on the bed and say, *I didn't sleep at all last night*, and Jolene would know exactly what she meant. The two of them would sit for hours, dissecting everything the guy had said or done. Back then they had both agreed that it wasn't any fun to get together with a guy if you didn't have a girlfriend to discuss it with.

But lately their allegiance has shifted some. They're still best friends, but there are things Jolene doesn't discuss with Carla anymore, things she knows Carla doesn't mention to her. It's easier for Jolene to talk to Leroy now.

"We came to see if y'all wanted to go on a picnic. Out to the Rock," she says.

"Okay with me." Carla shrugs her shoulders.

"Where's Jalapeño?" Leroy asks.

"Inside. We were out here drinking coffee when the phone rang. He's been on for a while." Carla jerks her head toward the door.

It smells like burned coffee inside the house. The television set is blaring from the messy living room, the floor is carpeted with newspapers. Leroy looks through the living room toward the kitchen. Jalapeño is crouched on a stool at the kitchen table, his shoulders hunched protectively, the phone against his ear. He looks toward the doorway. Leroy mouths *I'll be in the living room* and walks over to the sofa. He picks up Jalapeño's beat-up box guitar.

Even with the television on and a radio blasting from the bedroom, he can hear Jalapeño's end of the conversation. There is a silence, then Jalapeño asks: "Daddy, have you been to sleep at all? How long've you been up?" His voice is measured, patient, as if this is a conversation he has had before.

"Well, I don't think you should come down here," he says after a moment. "Everything is fine."

There is a longer pause and when he speaks again his voice is less calm. "Look, Daddy," he suggests. "I think you need some sleep. I've got people over. I don't have time to talk."

Leroy hears his sigh, all the way in the living room. "Yeah, right, Daddy," he says in a resigned voice. "You're absolutely right. Rome always falls. Why don't you just turn off CNN and get some sleep, all right?"

Leroy hears the click of the phone being set in its cradle. "Shit . . ." Jalapeño says and walks into the living room. "My old man." He looks at Leroy and shrugs his shoulders jerkily. "He's off the wagon. He called to tell me he'd made reservations for me on a plane to New Zealand."

"New Zealand? Does he have that kind of money?"

"Hell no. But he's got it in his head that New Zealand's the safest country we could be in." He sits down on the sofa.

"Oh, well," he sighs. "He'll forget he ever made the reservations. They'll cancel them, I guess." He pulls at the sofa's stuffing and stares at it. "My dad," he says slowly. "When he drinks, he sees plots, you know? I tell stories about it like I think it's funny, but it's really not. One night—I guess I was about fourteen and Danny was nine or ten—Daddy came sailing in our bedroom in his underwear. It's three o'clock in the morning, okay? He thinks the enemy's outside. So he pulls us out of bed and into the living room. There're empty wine bottles all over the floor and his rifle laying up against the sofa. See, he can hear them outside, rattling the bushes. I'm listening, but I can't hear a thing.

"We sit there a while and Daddy's in his chair with that gun across his lap. We're afraid to move, you know. He gets up and runs into the kitchen and comes back with a hammer and a box of nails. He's gonna nail those windows shut so nobody can get in.

"So there he is, an old, fat drunk running around in his underwear, nailing all those windows shut. Then he sort of calms down, and he's just sitting there in his recliner with his gun, his eyes closed. Stubble on his chin. It was getting white, you know?" Jalapeño looks at Leroy.

"I waited a long time," he says after a minute. "I got Danny back to bed and then I walked back in the living room and sat there watching Daddy. Waiting to see if his eyes were going to flicker, if he was going to wake back up. And then I finally figured he wasn't going anywhere till morning. I pulled the rifle off his lap and locked it in the closet.

"But when I was looking at him, I started seeing something I hadn't seen before. He looked *little*, in that chair with his mouth half-open. He looked old. He never beat on us. He'd get drunk as shit, but he'd never beat us. We thought he was a grown-up, that he knew what was going on. That night, it was the end of that, you know? I looked at him and started thinking that he didn't know shit about anything.

"It tore him up when Danny died. It almost killed him. I mean, that was later, but he always tried to look out for us. He'd come home and fix us supper. He couldn't cook at all, but every night he'd cook for us, set the table with the china mama left and real cloth napkins. He went to all those conferences at school, open-houses. I hated him because he'd go with his tool belt slung around his waist and his uniform still on. All I wanted was to be cut off from him." He stops. "I wanted to be all by myself, you know? I thought that would make it better."

Leroy picks at the guitar strings. He clears his throat. "Jolene wanted to know if y'all wanted to go on a picnic or something," he says.

"You already ask Carla?"

"She said it was okay with her." He looks at Jalapeño and Jalapeño looks back. "Bring your harmonica," Leroy suggests. "Then you can give us all a serenade."

Fourteen

Sometimes Leroy wonders if there are any families anywhere that are still together. Jolene's parents got divorced when she was little. And from the way Jalapeño talks, you wouldn't know he had a mother. Leroy's not sure about Carla; she's never mentioned anyone: brothers, sisters, any kind of family. He wouldn't even like her if he hadn't been able to get past her raspy voice and the high-heeled boots she wears enough to see that she's just trying to get by, living by herself in a bad apartment on a lousy side of town, and that all she has is Jolene, and maybe him, now that she's used to him.

It's not like Leroy's own home life was anything off a TV show. His grandmother, now, she loves him, it doesn't matter to *her* what he might have done. He could commit murder and she'd still be right behind him, like one of those women, the mothers of some convict that you see on *60 Minutes* sometimes, staring squarely at the camera and denying what everybody else can see is true. She's the one who might as well have raised him. She sent him candy, hidden in rolls of socks, when he was overseas. She was the one he took the time to write his letters to. She pieced the quilt he took with him. He never dreamed of telling her it sat in the bottom of his footlocker for four years—the army frowned on anything but olive-drab and regulation issue. She embroidered his full name square in the center in white, silky thread, the years of his service centered underneath. Jolene has commented that his quilt looks like something that should be draped over a coffin. The red and blue blocks of material sewn so neatly together. "Leroy" painstakingly done in embroidered script, and underneath it, "1980–1984."

Leroy's parents are different story. He talks to his mother maybe once a year, for fifteen minutes on Christmas Day. He never talks to his stepfather when he calls. His stepfather had sat down with him once, right after the wedding, and suggested Leroy call him Dad. Leroy knew his mother had put his stepfather up to it, he didn't really mean it. His stepfather's name was Darryl, but he had been "Bronco" when he was flying missions over Vietnam and it's "Bronco" he's remained. "Bronco loves wars," Leroy's told Jolene. "He's always disappointed when they end."

Bronco was the one who signed Leroy's papers so he could enlist before he finished high school.

"Maybe that'll make a man out of you," he told him. His voice was full of gritty satisfaction. Leroy stood in front of him, staring out the window behind his stepfather's shoulder. Fine, brown hair curled over the collar of his faded blue-jean jacket. He thought of being somewhere else, somewhere hot and sandy, where he'd be nothing but part of some gigantic machine, someplace where he'd be nothing but sweat and scoured clean. Bronco looked at him with narrowed eyes.

"At least you'll end up with a haircut," he said, handing Leroy his papers.

In Special Forces they taught Leroy how to kill a man with his bare hands. It bothers Jolene more than it bothers him. "It was all hypothetical," he reassures her, but it makes her angry; these are things no one should even have to know about. Their phone number's unlisted. Leroy doesn't trust the government. He doesn't trust hardly anything but her and Jalapeño.

His hands have tiny freckles on the backs of them. He pulls them across the strings of his guitar carefully. They're loose and sure over the engine when he's working on the van. She doesn't know if they remember how to snap a wrist or break a back.

When he was seventeen, his parents thought he was too dumb for school and too much to deal with, so he went into the army. When he got leave, he and his buddies all went into town, to ugly bars and prostitutes. He wanted someone he could talk to but he had no idea just how to go about it. The girls he met, they fumbled with his belt and yanked him back into the dark parts of the alleys. He wanted to say something, but all they knew to do was fuck him. He gave them money. There were track marks on their arms, and he never knew who they were. They never knew his name. It was the tradition.

There are so many things it's easy to get lulled into. Jolene's shocked when she realizes they eat dinner in front of the TV set and what they're watching isn't fake, what they're seeing are dead bodies. And this is just the news. They raise their forks up to their lips. It's automatic. Everything is fine.

Fifteen

The Rock looms sullenly on the horizon. The Indians thought its windswept top was haunted. Leroy's always said it's dull, a chunk of boring rock, but then he'll stand away from Jolene, off at the top, and stare up at the sky. They've been up there when it's almost dark, and *she* believes it's haunted, the way the winds sigh through the boulders and move the puddles on the top.

"There it is," she says. Carla looks at it disinterestedly from the back seat, rubbing suntan lotion on her freckled shoulders.

"Good Lord," Jalapeño says suddenly, "that stuff smells *weird,*" and then the four of them get out of the van, stretching and staring at the curving summit.

"All right, men," Leroy drawls, his best John-Wayne, "let's get going."

At the top, they sit down on the pink granite and stare up at the bowl-shaped sky. A jet's vapor trail snakes across it. Jolene lies down, the rock warming her back through her shirt.

"This is nice," Carla says, sounding slightly surprised. She's never considered herself the nature type.

"What if we could find a place, as far away and empty as this, to live in?" Jolene asks suddenly. "Not on the Rock, I mean, but somewhere out here. A fallen-down old farmhouse? We could all live there," she says, "all of us, and anybody we wanted. We could live off the land, plant a garden. I could grow some roses . . ."

Leroy laughs wryly, restlessly, and narrows his eyes to stare at the land spreading at the foot of the Rock, the wiry grass blasted and dead brown.

"No living off the land here," he says. "You must be imagining some other country. New Zealand, maybe?" He laughs and scrambles to his feet. "I'm going to explore." He jerks his head toward the tumble of towering, jagged boulders. "Who's coming with me?"

Jolene stands up beside him, brushing off her Levi's. Jalapeño shakes his head.

"I think I'll stay with Jalapeño," Carla says. Leroy and Jolene look at one another.

"Okay." Leroy shrugs. "Don't y'all go eating up the sandwiches."

Sixteen

Although the rest of the dome of the Rock is smooth, the western side is fissured—huge, jagged, up-thrown boulders smashed together. Leroy stands in the shadows of a looming outcropping, peering down into a crevice. He slips through the crack in the two rocks, groping his way. Jolene takes a deep breath and follows him. The huge rocks are worn and satiny under her hands. She's thinking about snakes. The rock around them is dry and cool. She cranes her neck upward. The walls of rock lean toward each other, almost touching farther up. A patch of blue sky shows in the space between them. It's like standing at the bottom of a giant chimney.

"What if we can't get out?" she whispers. She imagines some rappeller, snaking his rope out and swinging down into this cave-y place fifty years from now. Stumbling over their polished white bones, gleaming dully in the dark.

"Good Lord, Jolene." Leroy's voice is deliberately loud. "You've got an overactive imagination." He pulls himself up the slope toward a crack in the rocks that leads out into the daylight, then reaches down to hoist her up beside him. She stands up, blinking in the sudden light.

Looking downward, she can see that the path along the face of the Rock is really just a succession of toothy boulders, stacked like stairs but not so close together. Behind them, the dome soars upward, almost vertical. Leroy starts down, jumping from one crag to the next. She follows slowly, sliding on the seat of her jeans, bloodying her knuckles when she clutches at the rocks on either side.

She clings to the closest boulder and stares at the empty space in front of her—an eight-foot leap and the distance down between the two rocks a dizzying thirty feet or more. Leroy, on the ledge on the other side, looks both close and far away, the distance between his rock and hers just enough to jump, if you were lucky, or just enough to miss, fingers scrabbling at the chipping powdery rock, if you weren't.

"Go ahead and jump," he cajoles, "it's easier than it looks." She slides toward the edge and looks down and across, feeling something snag at her back pocket.

"I don't think I can," she says. She shades her eyes and forces herself to stare down the drop-off, at the sharp fingers of rock, beneath them, at the bottom. She's glad there's nobody around to see the two of them; the way she's got her arms wrapped tightly around the rock, the way Leroy's leaned toward her.

"Don't think about it," he says. "Just do it. Smooth, one motion. I'll steady you on the other side." But she's already thought, already seen before her eyes, as if it had already happened, her flailing, ungraceful leap and Leroy's confused movement forward. The way she misses the ledge. Or the way it crumbles under her feet. Eight feet isn't much, she tells herself. You walk it in two seconds. But that isn't how it seems. The space gapes in front of her.

"I'll coach you through it," Leroy says.

"I don't think I can," she says again.

"Just don't think," he tells her. "Let your muscles take over." She shakes her head.

"The only other thing to do is go back up," he tells her. She cranes her neck and looks back at the vertical slope.

"Okay," she says finally. "Don't let me fall." She takes a breath. Her muscles are bunched, her legs tensed. A quick spring and she lands on her knees beside him. Her heart beats loudly. She looks back at the sloping rock.

Seventeen

The shadows thrown by the tumbled rocks are sharp and stretched. It was easier going down than coming back up. The palms of Jolene's hands are scraped raw.

"We should have said we'd meet them at the bottom," she says.

Leroy jerks his head toward two figures near a tangled scrub of live oak, too out of breath to talk. "That them?"

She peers in the direction he gestured. "Yeah," she says. "I think."

They walk toward the trees. Ahead of them, one body crumples to the ground. The other figure takes a jerky half-step back. It seems to happen in slow motion.

"Oh, Jesus," Leroy breathes. "Oh, sweet Jesus." They start running. Carla turns toward them. When they reach her, her face is blank, surprised. Jalapeño's eyes are rolled back, staring at the sky. Only the whites are showing. A bubble of saliva is at the corner of the twitching mouth, his arms and legs are flailing. His body bucks horribly, convulsed and curved.

"The wallet," Jolene shrieks. "Get your wallet." Leroy bends over Jalapeño's face, trying to turn him on his side, trying to keep his head from hitting rock. Jolene's fingers scrabble at his back pocket. By the time she pulls the wallet out, Jalapeño's body has relaxed. His eyes are closed. As the three of them crouch over him, his eyelids flicker. They are greased with sweat. Jolene holds Leroy's wallet tightly, foolishly, in her hands. Beside her, Carla is crying.

"I didn't know," she babbles. "I didn't think anything like this could happen."

Leroy pulls his jacket off and shoves it under Jalapeño's head. Jalapeño opens his eyes and stares up at them weakly. He tries to push himself up to a sitting position.

"Stay cool, man," Leroy whispers, pushing his head back against the jacket. "Take it easy. You had a seizure. Tell us what we need to do—should somebody go get help? A doctor?" Jalapeño shakes his head and turns his face away from them.

"No doctor," he mutters, and his voice is so low Leroy has to bend toward his bruised lips to catch it. "I'll be okay now . . ." He is crying. Leroy gently wipes the pinkish froth from his mouth with a corner of his T-shirt.

"It just happens sometimes," he whispers. "I hate people to see." He licks his lips. "I'm awful sorry."

It's absolutely quiet. A buzzard's black above them, caught by the wind like an empty bag. Theirs is the only car in the asphalt lot below. Another one moves silently down the line of road that leads toward the highway.

"I'm sleepy," Jalapeño says suddenly, plaintively, and they all stir, Leroy helping him up as they start down the slope.

"Do you have a Kleenex?" Carla whispers to Jolene. Her face is red and wet and she won't look at Jolene directly.

Jolene shakes her head. "No," she says. "I'm sorry." She knows Carla doesn't want her to know she's crying.

"It's going to be okay," she says, although she suddenly feels doubt that what she says could possibly be true. She bumps her shoulders against Carla's, anyway, to try to make her smile.

"I made a mistake," Carla whispers to her, staring at the back of Jalapeño's head.

"How do you mean?"

"It used to never matter, you know? I never felt a thing. But this was different. The way he told me everything."

The rock beneath their feet is slick and both of them stop talking.

The sun sets suddenly on the drive home. The mesquite and hills draw the last light like a magnet. In the almost-dark, the shoulder of the road looks like the surface of the moon. Jolene leans her cheek against the cold glass of the window and watches the faint outlines of the slopes outside.

Turning, she can see Carla's eyes shining from the back seat. They are like the deer's that was caught, startled, in her headlights when she was coming back from somewhere, late at night, not that long ago. At the last possible minute, the deer had swerved and leapt, nimbly, to the dark ditch running along the side of the road. The abrupt movement had left a feeling that stretched, taut as strung wire, between her and Leroy, who was close beside her on the seat.

She can't see Jalapeño's eyes at all. She guesses it's because they're closed. Carla's holding his hand. The van labors slightly as it crests a ridge. Off to the side of the highway, there's a snaking line of flame along the low curve of the horizon, silhouetting the bony fingers of the mesquite and brush beside it.

"Jesus," Jolene says, "what's that?" Carla stirs in the back seat. Jalapeño draws a deep breath.

"Grass fire, I guess," Leroy speculates. "Spooky-looking," he mutters. Jolene cranes her neck to watch the flames. The fire stretches toward the horizon. The low clouds above it are tinged with pink. The van hurtles down the highway.

When they hit town, Leroy points the van toward Jalapeño's run-down house without even asking. Jolene can tell by the stiff set of his shoulders how much Jalapeño's spell scared him.

"What's he doing?" he asks suddenly.

"Sleeping," Carla says, "just sleeping."

He turns off the interstate and cuts through the neighborhood bordering Jalapeño's. The houses are dark, except for the glow from an occasional television set. Manicured lawns roll away from the square, ranch-style houses. Through the van's open window, Jolene can hear the soft swish of their tires against pavement. Yellow plastic ribbons flutter from the mailboxes at the ends of the identical driveways.

The closer they get to Jalapeño's house, the more the neighborhood deteriorates. The cars in the driveways are propped up on cement blocks; harsh yellow light spills from open doorways. Passing one house, there's the sound of music, a sudden surge that quickly fades away behind them. Leroy noses the van to the curb in front of Jalapeño's house.

Carla touches Jalapeño tentatively, shaking his shoulder. He unfolds his long legs and moves his head groggily. Leroy gets out and walks around to the passenger door, opening it and making a move as if to help him out.

He stands up unsteadily, grasping at the door frame. He peers back into the van, blinking.

"Why don't y'all come in for a while," he says brightly. The car-door light illuminates them. Leroy's hand is frozen on his shoulder. Jolene and Carla's faces are turned toward them.

"We could buy some beer or something," he starts off. "We could get some food . . ." He wavers on his feet. "Please stay just a little while."

At the front door he fumbles with his key for the lock. "We could watch the war on my new TV," he tells them, pushing open the front door.

They move into the darkness blindly, and it seems cold and quiet, absolute. Jalapeño staggers slightly and leans against the door. Jolene turns and Carla lunges toward him. Leroy, closest, puts an arm around him. The four of them huddle in the doorway, and in the dark their shoulders bump; they are leaning close together, trying hard to keep their feet.

Grand Portage

*I*n some of the states, livestock was the only thing on the horizon. The two of them drove in shifts; the states got flatter. In Kansas, they sped past a looming billboard of a cow prancing on its hind legs, wearing lipstick and pearl jewelry. EAT MORE BEEF was written underneath. The cows bunched beside the sign's stilt-legs looked unconcerned. They flung up puzzled heads and stared out at the stretched-out rubber band that was the highway. An eighteen-wheeler lumbered toward the Monte Carlo, tiny on the horizon as a bug. The rounded hills were solid and hunched as sleeping cattle.

First Errol would drive and Delilah would wriggle on the seat and say, *Slow down,* and then they would switch places and he would look over at the speedometer and say, *You're going to get a ticket.* By the time they were in Kansas, they were on some sort of turnpike and the road was almost empty. They didn't see a single cop, and Delilah decided she had it figured out. Instead of issuing speeding tickets, the Kansas State Patrol just made you pay to use their road. Everybody knew the money earned from traffic tickets was used to maintain highways. You didn't get tickets, she explained to Errol, because you broke some kind of moral law. On the turnpike, you just got the money-spending part over with and were free to drive the way you wanted. A rusted-out Charger barreled past them as if to bear her theory out.

"I don't think that would be a safe assumption to make," Errol warned her, slouched down in the seat, muttering toward the inside of his grubby fleece-lined jacket. "I don't think that would be a safe assumption to make at all." But then he fell asleep, his head squashed up against the window, and didn't know she was swooping up the sleepy hills at over ninety. It was almost dark and his face seemed tired and pointed behind the huge reflecting lenses of his sunglasses, but Delilah was driving so fast she couldn't turn her head to look at him for very long.

Delilah had felt happy when they sped across the border into Oklahoma, just because they'd crossed it. It wasn't until then that she stopped being afraid Donny's motorcycle would be behind them if she turned her head around. Oklahoma's rest stops were run-down and smelled of dirty diapers. She held her breath inside the tiny, scratched-up stall. GOODBYE TEXAS, HELLO NOTHING proclaimed a frantic set of words gouged into the wall. In Oklahoma the red dirt along the interstate was eroded into jagged planes: if she squinted she could tell herself they were in a strange, exotic landscape; although if she kept her eyes open, she could see that Oklahoma looked about the same as Texas except there were more horses grazing in the fields along the shoulder of the road. Outside Oklahoma City the three lanes of the northbound interstate were crowded with shiny Japanese-made pickup trucks.

"Oklahoma City?" she asked Errol, looking at the exit sign. The buildings of the city loomed off in the distance, poking up from the flat ground.

Oklahoma was the first day; Errol had been driving then. "Not yet," he told her. "Let's get a little farther." Neither of them wanted to stop, both of them still thinking of the way they'd left Donny by the rutted driveway with the wreckage of the things he'd smashed stacked up neatly at the curb beside him.

"You weasel," he had said to Errol. He wouldn't look at Delilah and she just looked down toward her feet. "You fucking little weasel," Donny said. Delilah kept her eyes lowered toward the inside of the Monte Carlo, the crumpled paper from a pack of cigarettes and an empty beer bottle that had rolled up from underneath the seat and rested by her ankle, the ankle that had *Donny* arched in ink across it, the letters so big they almost wrapped around it like a chain. Errol threw the car into reverse and she wouldn't look behind her, although she couldn't help but move her eyes toward the rearview mirror to watch the spindly mimosa tree beside the driveway recede. The scraped gash where Donny's work van had hit it was almost hidden from her view by his body. He stood facing out toward the street as if he still nursed close an expectation that the car would swing into a U-turn and she would open up the door and look at him and say, *I changed my mind.* He had knocked that scar into the tree the morning he was late to work, the morning after that first night he hadn't gone to bed at all, the morning she had walked into the bathroom and seen the needle sitting on the little ledge above the sink. Delilah couldn't remember exactly when that morning had been. It seemed like a long time ago.

They stopped for gas at a Stuckey's across the Oklahoma border. It wasn't close to anything. Delilah stood in front of a revolving wire stand and looked vacantly out the dirty plate-glass window, fanning a sheaf of postcards of things that didn't look like they could possibly be in Oklahoma. Errol was outside, filling up the car with gas. She had no idea what she would write down on a postcard if she were to buy one. *I'm in Oklahoma. I broke up with Donny. I'm with a guy named Errol now; we're on the way to Canada.* A sagging string was tacked along the wall beside the postcard rack. MY WIFE RAN OFF WITH MY BEST FRIEND; I SURE DO MISS HIM lamented one of the baseball caps clothespinned to the string. She walked out of the building and stood beside the car.

"You'll be sorry," Donny had shouted at her. What had there been for her to say to him, when he finally asked her? "You'll be awfully fucking sorry," he had said. She knew he was right.

She decided it was interesting: the way you could know something for so long and still convince yourself it wasn't true. "I kicked that stuff," Donny had sworn when he first met her. His face was earnest above the collar of his striped uniform shirt. His name was sewn above the left-hand pocket. He told her that a girl had introduced him to it, outside a bar in Houston. But that had been a while ago. He didn't need it now. Delilah told him she would leave him if she ever knew. It was hard to make her mouth shape the words. If she knew that he was shooting drugs. She didn't think it would happen. That was when his face was young and almost happy-looking and she was not suspicious about anything. Later on was when the flesh around his eyes got puffy and he was always tired. She felt somehow responsible. He had seemed fine when she had met him. It must have been something she had done that caused it all: the relationship's decline.

The second morning, after she and Errol pulled out of the parking lot outside the motel, when it was still so early that the fields they passed seemed green and washed-off, clean, she started asking questions. He didn't want to answer.

That one night, when he and Donny had gone off for a beer and Donny had come back home at four-thirty in the morning—had Donny been shooting up then? Had Errol done it too? Was that what they did those nights they went out—to play pool, they said—when she stayed home because she thought that pool was sort of a stupid game and sometimes she just wanted to be away from Donny, to have the house all to herself, and maybe it was good for him to have a guy friend to hang out with? And then there had been the bruises on the insides of Donny's arms that he had said he got at work somehow, but now she saw how it had really been—she had been so fucking stupid. Her voice spiraled upward, higher, and Errol eased the Monte Carlo over to the shoulder of the road. The car shook every time a truck moved past, and she stared out the window dully. He pushed the sleeves back on his shirt.

"Look," he said. He stretched his arms, turned up, toward her. "I waited in the car. The nights he went and got it." A truck moved up in front of them.

"You could have tried to stop him," she mumbled.

"Look," he said again gently. "One night he told me that he loved it—more than anything."

"I never should have *been* with him," she said. "I never should have gone ahead and moved right in. I should have never even *talked* to him." She pressed her hands up to her eyes.

"You did what you could," he said. She looked out the window and didn't reply because it was the same thing he'd been saying since the night when everything had happened, and although it had soothed her then, it suddenly seemed meaningless. Suddenly, she had no idea what it was that she was doing or how it was she had ended up in Errol's ugly, rusted Monte Carlo, a car that would never, she suddenly believed, make it half as far as Grand Portage, where his father was and where he was intent on going.

She hadn't meant for any of it to happen. Or maybe that wasn't really true, maybe she *had*. The three of them had done almost everything together. She sat between them when they went to the movies. Errol had been at the house the night Donny stood up from the couch abruptly and said he was going for a pack of cigarettes, and it was Errol who went out and looked for him at four in the morning when Delilah started crying because he still had not come back.

Somewhere in there she had started looking at Errol differently. Somewhere between the first jerky, angry gesture Donny made, the star-shaped hole he punched into the wall above the bed, and that final awful moment—when he looked at her and said quietly, *I guess you have to leave now, don't you?*—everything had changed.

In the Jesse James Museum there was a clump of brownish hair laid under glass, right next to a display of Jesse's boots. "He must have been a little guy," Delilah whispered. The boots were short and stubby. Photographs of Frank and Jesse James stared down from the walls. Jesse's face was babyish, but his eyes were flat and opaque, shallow. "It doesn't say a thing about how many people he killed," Delilah pointed out. She stared at the pair of boots. She thought of Jesse's little feet. The photograph on the wall hung like a lizard, and outside there were cicadas and the August heat. "This place gives me the creeps," she said.

The hair inside the case was a match, the hand-written card next to it assured them, with the hair of Jesse James. A lumpy woman in a red-and-black-striped tube top bent toward it, chewing gum, her face disbelieving. Errol stood in front of a display enclosed behind a plate of glass smeared with sweaty fingerprints. The chair Jesse had been standing on when he was shot was placed against the wall. The picture he had been dusting when he died hung just above it. The feather duster that had slipped from his hand was lying on the floor. The picture was still a little crooked on the wall. It said: IN GOD WE TRUST. It was as if the most important moment remained frozen: a little man pulling a chair out from the table because he wasn't tall enough to reach the crooked, cross-stitched maxim hanging on the wall. They'd been planning that last bank job when Jesse rose to straighten up the picture on the wall. He had just sworn that it was going to be the final job. All he needed was this last bank and then there'd be the money for the farm, the retreat to Nebraska. The details were the touch that made you sympathize: the fact that he was short, that he was shot in the back of the head, that this was going to be *the last time*. It was in his death that James became important because it cut things off so cleanly. You didn't have to know that even though he loved his mother his eyes were flat and cruel. It was easy to believe that robbing banks was something he just stopped or started when he wanted to, a habit that hurt no one, a way to make a living. Errol stared at the display for a long time, even after Delilah turned toward him and opened her mouth to say something and then closed it again. She moved into the gift shop. It was a small one: Missouri didn't seem to have too much to offer. There were coffee cups emblazoned with the likenesses of the James brothers, Confederate flag license plates, and a row of thumbed-through postcards. Delilah selected two jiggers engraved with a picture of the gang.

"Maybe your dad'll like them," she suggested when they were walking through the parking lot. She pulled them out of the paper bag. "I thought maybe we should take something. Something little. You know, like a hostess present." Errol hardly looked at them.

"I have no idea," he said. He seemed jittery, standing by the car while she unlocked the door. He opened his wallet. "We'll be sleeping in the car, I guess," he said. "We've been spending too much money." Delilah turned the Monte Carlo back onto the highway, and he huddled against the passenger side door grimly. He reached across her for the photograph paper clipped to the sun visor and tilted it toward the windshield.

All this flatness, he said suddenly, made him agoraphobic. It had been so long since he had said anything that Delilah was startled. They were in Iowa now.

"Afraid to leave the house?" she questioned.

"Afraid of something," he replied. "I don't know what." He carefully set the photograph up on the dash, against the heater vent. The three tiny blurred faces bobbed against the windshield. The man's teeth were tiny, brilliant white. He leaned up against a car, a beer in one hand, the other around the woman who was tilted toward him, staring up into his face. Even with her beehive, she hardly came up to his chin. She grasped at the shoulder of the little boy, turning him so he was forced between them. It wasn't in the picture, but Errol's brown and white terrier had been chained to the clothesline behind that house. In Amarillo, the hot wind had blown continuously. Errol had been five. Two weeks after the picture, the terrier had run out into traffic. In a year, the smiling man had disappeared.

"Maybe we should call him before we get there," Delilah said.

It was family values all through Iowa. That and "Suspicious Minds." It was the fifteenth anniversary of Elvis's death. It was the Republican Convention. They drove through one bad AM station into the next, the Monte Carlo fishtailing across the center line and back when Errol gave up on the static and tried to change the station. "I don't understand this," he said finally. "Why is 'Suspicious Minds' the only song they ever play?" The first time had been early in the morning and they had sung along. The inside of the car filled up with empty coffee cups. Errol drummed his fingers on the steering wheel. On the radio a minister informed them they were in God's Country. Errol switched to another station. When they stopped for gas, the sleeve of his T-shirt blew back past the tiny tattoo on his biceps. The men lingering by the cash register stared, and Delilah knew that neither of them represented *family values*.

In Iowa, they stopped to eat cinnamon rolls the size of plates at a low, flat building that stretched beside the interstate. They stopped for the night at a rest stop on the far side of the Minnesota border. The rest stop was set back from the highway and when the wind moved through the trees outside the car, they sounded different from the trees in Texas. When Delilah lay down, her head was trapped beneath the steering wheel. Errol stretched out in the back seat. Halfway through the night he started shouting. He sat up on the seat and stared through the windshield blankly. The vapor lights along the shoulder lit up the access road like a tunnel and beyond that, behind the screen of pale birch trees, the semis whined and clashed their gears and rumbled past. Delilah leaned over the seat. She touched his hand. "Everything's okay," she said. The car smelled of the apple she had eaten in the afternoon and stuffed into the ashtray. Her voice sounded peculiar. Errol shook his head and climbed over the seat. They huddled against the passenger-side door.

"It gets awfully cold at night here," he said after a while.

In Minnesota, the air smelled different. The sun went away halfway through the morning and then the Monte Carlo labored up a steady rise and crested it and on the other side Duluth clung to a piece of land shaped like a bowl with Lake Superior in the middle of it. The city was the color of coal and dirty pavement, and the lake spread out like slate. There wasn't any land on the horizon.

"It looks just like the ocean," Delilah whispered. The sudden sight of it made her stomach sink. Errol eased his foot off the accelerator.

"Jesus," he said slowly. The highway hung suspended above a long expanse of empty buildings. In the distance it divided into cabled, fragile-looking bridges—*the longest in the country*, the atlas exclaimed—that arched off toward the gray horizon. Errol ignored exits and kept going straight. The highway jolted down to street level and turned into an intersection rubbing up against the shoreline, with a blinking streetlight.

"What happened to the interstate?" he asked. Delilah looked down at the map.

"That's it, I guess. We went from one end to the other." The thought amazed her. She looked from the map to the window and back again.

"These houses look strange," she commented after a while. Errol was hunched over the steering wheel.

"I don't like them," he said flatly. The gables were too sharp and pointy. The fronts were long and skinny and faced toward the lake. "I like a house that spreads out." These houses were hardly up above the water line. They looked unsafe to him, he said. He was forgetting Lake Superior was not an ocean. That they were in a place where the concern was cold, not hurricanes.

The Monte Carlo took them past motels and pie stands. The engine started to sound labored. The Water's Edge. The Surf-Side Lodge. The motels were tiny, wooden houses huddled close together with the dark brush and trees behind them and the sullen lake across the road. Each motel-house seemed to have a fireplace and curtains hanging in the windows.

"Could we stay in one of those?" Delilah asked. She leaned her head out the window and her hair snaked back inside the car. She had been more cheerful since they got off the interstate. She reached inside the bag of Old Dutch potato chips they'd bought at the last gas station. She peered back at every roadside stand they passed. She wanted to buy guidebooks, smoked salmon, tiny, rounded jars of something labeled pumpkin butter.

"If it doesn't cost too much," Errol said.

She bounded out of the car every time they stopped for a scenic overlook. He followed slowly when they stopped to stare out across a drop-off at a spitting waterfall that ran into the lake. He hunkered his shoulders inside his dirty jacket. "This is nice," Delilah said. She leaned precariously over the iron railing and peered down at the falls. Her eyes were bright. He shrugged.

"What's wrong?" she asked him.

"I don't know," he said. "I'm not sure I like it here. It's almost like another country."

"It's just because there isn't any sun today." She tugged at his hand.

"Maybe," he said finally and she looked at him closely, knowing what he was thinking, wanting to say, *Maybe you should just call him and tell him that we're coming.*

They stopped for the night at the last town before the Indian reservation and the border. Delilah looked down at the map. It was the first town they had gone through since Duluth big enough to have its name in larger, darker type. Errol swerved off the highway at a sign and pulled into a graveled driveway. "Okay?" he asked.

It was four o'clock. "It's only fifty more miles," she said. "We could get there tonight." Errol was silent. He wouldn't look at her directly.

"Look," he finally mumbled. "I want to change, to shave and shower first. I want," he told her slowly, "to look presentable."

The cabins were miniature white-painted houses lined up in a row behind a mobile home set into a gouged place cut into the mountain that loomed beside the lake. The honeymoon cabin was the only one with television. "You *are* married?" the man who emerged from the trailer said before he pulled the key down from a hook next to the front door. Delilah was too sleepy to think to shove the hand that would have had a wedding band into her pocket.

"Of course," Errol told him. The light glinted off the thick lenses of the man's glasses as he turned to stare at the Monte Carlo's license plate. "Checkout time is nine o'clock," he told them. "God speed to you both," he said.

The paneled walls were decorated with pictures torn from magazines. The darker knotholes in the walls made Delilah think of eyes. *God loves you,* the print on a picture of a rainbow arched above a majestic mountain said. *Jesus Saves!* announced a water-stained picture tacked beside the bathroom sink. Errol closed the drapes and drank a warm beer he'd gotten some miles back, and then he hid the empty bottle in the suitcase. "So the religious motel-guy won't know," he explained. Delilah felt like there was someone outside the windows, watching. After dark, the row of cabins was cocooned in quiet, as if it had sunk down to the bottom of the brooding lake. Errol slept beside her, huddled underneath the scratchy blanket. There wasn't the sound of anything and suddenly she knew she wasn't ever going to fall asleep.

Was it adultery when you weren't even married? Delilah hadn't thought of it like that, although she knew it was. It was the kind of thing she'd sworn she'd never do. After Donny found out, he threatened to tell everyone—her boss, he raved; he'd write her grandmother; he'd tell their next-door neighbor. It shamed her more than anything. "You kept going off and leaving us together," she tried to explain.

He looked at her stonily.

"I'm sorry," she said. "I didn't mean for it to happen."

"Was it," he said wildly, "when I broke that window? Was that what made it happen? I told you I was sorry." He *had*, and she had acted like it was okay, but now she knew it wasn't really, that under everything they had ever tried to renegotiate had been the nights when doors had slammed so hard the windows shook. The fists through glass. The ripped shirt where he grabbed her when she turned toward the door. The workless days. She had said she had, but she had not forgiven. They had become bound together by something with a tighter hold than love. They approached each other conspiratorially. All that really mattered was that the neighbors never hear.

"You'll never tell," Donny had stated matter-of-factly, early on. For awhile she thought she never would. It was even hard to say it to the cops, the night the neighbors called them. It seemed to bore them when she started crying. They wanted to know what she had done. "A new boyfriend?" one speculated. There wasn't a new boyfriend then. She shook her head. They looked down at their notepads when she had to blow her nose.

"Take pictures if he leaves a mark," they told her.

Delilah hadn't known Errol had packed a suit; she hadn't even known he owned one. When they loaded up the car, it was barely dawn and his face was cleanly shaven. He moved nervously toward the car and back. She noticed there was white dog hair on his suit coat and that his shoes needed to be polished.

"Are you nervous?" She touched his arm.

"Fuck no," he said. He slipped his arm away. They drove in silence. The lake was hidden by fog; it rolled in the low places on the road. *Mount Josephine*, a sign directed, pointing upward. The road climbed up; there was jagged cliff on one side and the lake on the other, and then the road dipped down.

The first time, they sped past the place without seeing it and drove until they were confronted with the customs station at the border. They had assumed his father lived in a town.

"Maybe we went too far," Delilah suggested. Errol wrenched the car around and drove back to the gas station that had been the only building they had passed in miles. He got out of the car and walked up to the cash register and toyed with a display of fishhooks lined up on the counter.

"I'm looking for a man," he said. He cleared his throat. "I'm looking for a man named Cyril Jones."

There was a nondescript-looking dog in the rutted mud that seemed to be the driveway, but it didn't bark, and a half-built house facing the road with a trailer catty-corner to it. Errol turned the key in the ignition. His shoulders slumped over the steering wheel. "What if I came back out and got you in a minute?" he said finally.

"Sure," she said. He straightened his shoulders as he walked toward the trailer. She wondered if he noticed the tipped-over Big Wheel next to the front door. He raised his fist up to the door and knocked. A woman answered, paused, and led him through the door. Delilah stared toward the trailer. The sun swung higher. The wind sighed through the topmost branches of the trees. Beyond the trailer, a stand of quaking aspens shivered, and on the road sometimes a car sped past. At one point, it was a UPS truck, and Delilah wondered sleepily where it had come from so early in the morning and so far away from anything. The inside of the car was warm, and she pulled off her sweater and leaned her head against the window.

Then Errol was tapping on the glass with his hand. His blue eyes, usually light-colored, were tired and without expression, darkened almost black.

"Why don't you come inside," he said, "and meet my dad before we leave." His voice was noncommittal. She looked at him and started to say something, but they were at the trailer door.

The inside of the trailer seemed moist and smelled of soured milk and coffee and too many cigarettes smoked so early in the morning. There was a baby crying in the other room, and a dark-skinned woman with a bad permanent was sitting at the kitchen table raising a lighter up toward her cigarette.

Errol's father looked like him, but there was something else in his expression, something bland and nervous at the same time, something somehow untouched by the fact that Errol, twenty-two years older than the last time he'd laid eyes on him, was standing in the middle of his living room. He was falsely jovial.

"A long trip," he said loudly. "And what led you to this neck of the woods?" Delilah looked at Errol and he looked back at her grimly. She said something vague about wanting to see that part of the country. Errol was silent. He suddenly reached across the table for the woman's pack of cigarettes and shook one from it. His father addressed remarks toward Delilah. Telling her he'd heard that things were bad in Texas now. He guessed it must be real different than it'd been when he had left it. Just what had they thought of Lake Superior? He looked past her out the tiny kitchen window, his eyes veering away from Errol where he sat at the kitchen table, turning the lighter over and over slowly in his hands.

Errol stood up abruptly. "Well," he said. His father was clumsy when he moved toward the table. He and Errol shook hands stiffly. Errol was awkward and solemn in his wrinkled suit. He kept his eyes cast down. Delilah wished they were somewhere else, on the highway in the Monte Carlo, traveling somewhere full of expectation. *Everybody needs their family,* she had told him when he'd said he was thinking of driving up to Grand Portage. What exactly had she known about it? And who was she to say when it was finally time to turn your back?

She and Errol moved toward the door. His father ducked into the other room. He came back with some folded bills he pressed into Errol's hand. The woman at the table turned her head and frowned and lit another cigarette.

"It was nice to meet you," Errol said. The woman nodded in acknowledgment, but for a second Delilah wondered if the words had been directed at her or at his father. No one looked at them and said, *We'd love to have you back.* Errol didn't say, *I'll write*, his father didn't say, *If I've got something for you, where is it I should send it?*

"Take care of yourselves," his father told them heavily.

"Are you okay?" she asked him. He laid his arm across the top of the seat and craned his head around, backing the Monte Carlo out of the driveway. The dog watched them from the edge of it, nose tilted up toward the sky. The trailer door was tightly closed. Errol didn't answer.

"My mother used to tell me about when she met him," he said finally. "How she was just a kid and he'd stop by every night and they'd go driving. And she'd hope they caught every red light, coming back to the house. That way it'd take them longer. He'd always bitch, because he had to let go of her hand to shift the gears. And then one night, he drives up and he's moved the shifter to the left-hand side. So he won't have to let go of her hand.

"All this time—years!—I've had some picture of him in my head. It didn't have to do with anything. And then, when we were sitting in that kitchen suddenly all I was thinking was how the fuck do you move a gearshift like that? Was it manual or automatic? Was it just some shit my mom made up? When I was little, I thought it meant he must have really loved her." He shrugged. "Long way for nothing, right?"

Delilah put her hand on his thigh and he swung the car heavily onto the road, headed northward. LAST AMERICAN GAS, a billboard announced. DUTY-FREE STORE. The highway curved away from the lake toward some buildings clustered underneath a sign that said: CANADIAN BORDER ¼ MILE. Errol turned the car toward them. He parked and strode across the asphalt.

"He gave me a hundred dollars," Errol said. They were standing in front of the plate-glass window, staring through it at the liquor bottles and cartons of cigarettes and bottles of perfume lined up inside against the wall. There was a slot machine next to the front door and a pay phone that was out of order. "We could just drink it up," he said. "Or gamble." Delilah looked closely at his reflection in the window.

"I guess we could," she said. She turned away from him, toward a rack of brochures nailed to the wall beside the door. He followed her and picked one up.

"We could rent a boat," he said. He jerked his head toward the lake across the highway. "Do something fun." He pulled the folded twenties out of his pocket. "It's not like I'm going to save it."

The boat hovered; the tour guide killed the engine.

"That's it," he said. He pointed. "The wreck of the *America*. Six feet under water here, sixty at the other end." The water was light green, and the sunlight slicing through it traveled over something dark and mossy, something metal, huge, that sloped down gently into the depths they couldn't quite make out. Errol leaned toward the water and Delilah started to, but then she jerked back suddenly because the hull of the boat was so thin, a brittle piece of something—fiberglass?—and it was all there was between them and the water. Something about the wide sky, the pointing pines that ringed it, the sagging empty dock the boat had idled past, and the water underneath them scared her, as if they were in danger of snagging on something, a twisted piece of metal, wire, rope, an anchor. It didn't matter to her that the boat took every group of tourists past the wreck.

"How deep does it get?" she asked. "The lake?"

"About six hundred feet." The tour guide looked at her. "Gives a funny feeling, doesn't it?" He gestured toward the water. "Of course there weren't any casualties on the *America*, just a dog tied up below. The *Edmund Fitzgerald*, though? It went down with twenty-nine people. Still there."

Errol stirred. He raised his head from where he stared at the water off the bow. "What do you mean, still there?" he said.

"The water's so cold, you know," the tour guide explained. "And there aren't many scavengers in Lake Superior."

"How awful," Delilah said. Errol recoiled from where he bent toward the water. He moved toward her, took her hand.

"Good fishing here," the tour guide said wistfully. "But then you said you didn't want to fish." He started up the engine.

Delilah and Errol leaned toward each other, clumsy in their padded life vests, and Errol shivered slightly when he squeezed her hand. "Where to now?" he asked.

Delilah looked up at him for a second. "Home, I guess," she said.

They turned and stared out at the shining water, eyes on the boat's wide wake, the wrecks that lurked beyond it, and the things below, down in the dark, the things that caught you by the sleeve, the hair; things that hissed, like fishing line cast out, *remember*, and held until you drowned.

UNIVERSITY PRESS OF NEW ENGLAND

publishes books under its own imprint and is the publisher for Brandeis University Press, Dartmouth College, Middlebury College Press, University of New Hampshire, Tufts University, and Wesleyan University Press.

ABOUT THE AUTHOR

Katherine L. Hester's fiction has been published in *Prize Stories: The O. Henry Awards 1994*, *The Indiana Review*, *Cimarron Review*, and *American Short Fiction*. She attended the University of Georgia and the University of Texas at Austin, and has been the recipient of a James A. Michener Fellowship in Writing and a fellowship to the MacDowell Colony. A native of Texas, she now lives in Frankfurt, Germany.

LIBRARY OF CONGRESS CATALOGING-IN-PUBLICATION DATA

Hester, Katherine L.
    Eggs for young America / Katherine L. Hester.
      p.   cm.
    "The Katharine Bakeless Nason literary publication prizes."
    ISBN 0–87451–823–7 (alk. paper)
    I. Title.
PS3558.E79793E38   1997
813'.54—dc21   97–1758